MAXINE CHERNOFF'S

BOP

"These stories display an intelligent playfulness and a fine,
inventive talent. Chernoff's plots lead us places we don't ex-
pect to go—the prose is full of surprising, odd turns and
glimpses into the sad, wacky undersides of character."

—JOAN SILBER,
author of *Household Words*
and *In The City*

"Chernoff's is a Chicago sensibility—warm but skeptical,
worldly but down-to-earth."

—JAMES ATLAS

"*Bop* is a triumph for any reader lucky enough to live in it."

—JAYNE ANNE PHILLIPS

STORIES BY MAXINE CHERNOFF

BOP

VINTAGE CONTEMPORARIES
Vintage Books
A Division of Random House
New York

FIRST VINTAGE CONTEMPORARIES EDITION, ·
September 1987

Copyright © 1986 by Maxine Chernoff

Library of Congress Cataloging-in-Publication Data
Chernoff, Maxine, 1952–
Bop : stories.
(Vintage contemporaries)
I. Title.
PS3553.H356B6   1986b   813'.54   87-40070
ISBN 0-394-75522-7 (pbk.)

These stories have appeared in the following magazines: "Bop" in *TriQuarterly,* "Degan Dying" in *City,* "Don't Send Poems, Send Money" in *Playgirl,* "Enough" in *Oyez Review,* "Heroes" in *Kansas Quarterly,* "The Hills of Andorra" in *North American Review,* "Phantom Pleasure" in *Another Chicago Magazine,* "Respect for the Dead" in *Uncle,* "The Spirit of Giving" in *North American Review,* and "That Summer" in *The Iowa Review.*

"The Spirit of Giving" was chosen for the P.E.N. Syndicated Fiction Project in 1985.

The author thanks the Illinois Arts Council, a State agency, for artist grants in 1983, 1984, and 1985.

Author photo copyright © 1987 by Carole Harmel

Manufactured in the United States of America
10   9   8   7   6   5   4   3   2   1

CONTENTS

For Julian, Philip, Koren, and always for Paul

THE SPIRIT
OF GIVING

MY SISTER COLLECTS primitive art, so on her birthday I
sent her an Eskimo calendar. Each month shows a different
block print of Eskimos hunting, sitting around a fire, or
stretching seal skins on frames. The prints are done in rich
primary colors. They are striking in their simplicity. After
the year is over, the prints are suitable for framing.

My sister and I are close. Although she lives in San Francisco, we talk several times a month. When I didn't hear
from her for three weeks after I'd sent the gift, I decided to
call her.

"I hate it," she said on the phone in a nervous voice. "I
know it's unkind of me to tell you, but I'm used to speaking
the truth. The prints are finely executed, but I hate what's
omitted. All the blood spilled, all the flesh rendered."

"I should have sent you photos of bok choy," I suggested.
"Or of a tribe that only eats dead bumblebees they find in
the grass. It's life, Martha."

"I know," she answered. "Who's the anthropologist?"

She is. We talked about other things – Andy, the kids, nu-
clear war. Then she told me she had to go to her stained-
glass workshop. Seemed she was in hot pursuit of a hum-
mingbird.

After the call I went back to my desk to write her a letter.
I asked her how it felt to be such a sentimentalist. I questioned her own studies of primitive art, if much of it isn't
sacrifice and blood, even human blood spilled to assure
favor. I never sent the letter.

Two months later I was looking through those shopping

9

catalogues I get in the mail, the ones from famous Texas gift stores. Last year I could have bought a ticket to ride on the first space shuttle to carry passengers or an oil painting by Richard Nixon called "Boats Escaping, Retirement Years." I opted for a new bathrobe of green velour. I bought Ted some sheepskin earmuffs he never wore. In fact, when I gave them to him, he said, "You have to be kidding, Jane. I'm a translator!"

"Maybe you wanted a plastic replica of the Rosetta stone?" I asked. Our relationship has gone downhill since. Sometimes we meet for pasta and Chianti, but our conversations are strained.

This Christmas I'm determined to choose gifts with more care. Martha still hasn't forgiven me, though her humming-bird was a success. She sold it at a small art fair for a hundred twenty-six dollars and fifty cents. The fifty cents might have discouraged customers, but she's uncompromising.

First I consider gift certificates, but they're safe as white bread. Then I call a friend and ask her what she buys for her sister. "House slippers. My sister loves house slippers. This year I bought her a pair monogrammed MM. I found them in an art-deco shop."

"Are those her initials?"

"Marilyn Monroe. They're her initials. I thought my sister would get a kick out of wearing Marilyn Monroe's slippers."

My friend is no help. My sister would call me uncaring. "That poor woman died in her bed. Some people even say she was murdered. How sad to own the slippers in which she thought her last thoughts."

A few nights later I'm reading a journal of aging. As we all know, the Eskimos used to leave their elderly to die on ice floes. The old took it in good spirits, but even so. Now it's more popular to have the elderly move in with unmarried daughters, who not only care for them in their illness but if they have no teeth, chew the tough and gristly seal meat for them.

That night I dream I'm a young Eskimo woman with very strong teeth. My job is to chew seal meat not only for my parents but for my in-laws, my great-aunt Ida, who has red hair in my dream, and her pet retriever, Yuk-Yuk. When I wake up, my jaws ache, and I remember it's December seventeenth. If I don't send Martha a present soon, I'll have to send her an apology.

When I get home that night from dinner with Ted, this time moo-shoo pork in a crowded basement in Chinatown, I call Martha.

"Did you ever eat moo-shoo pork?" I ask.

"It looks like chewed food. I don't like it," she says.

How is it that my sister always knows my thoughts and critiques them before they're announced?

"Did you know that Eskimos no longer let their parents die on ice floes? Rather, they chew the food for their toothless elders and care for them the rest of their lives."

"The job usually falls to the unmarried daughter," she adds, meaning me.

"That's right! I'd be the one chewing the food."

Martha chortles. I can hear Andy in the background telling the kids not to paint on the white rug.

"How are you and Ted?" she asks.

"He didn't like the earmuffs I gave him."

"Speaking of presents," she says, "I sent you a purse I got at an ethnic fair. It's from China. It shows a duck hiding in some rushes while a feast is taking place in the palace to the left. I thought it wonderfully humorous."

"Did you ever think," I ask her, "how nothing is funny except predation? Think of cartoons, the roadrunner eluding the coyote, Bugs Bunny hiding from Elmer Fudd. The punch line is 'You can't eat me.'"

"You're deep, Jane." We say goodbye soon after.

The next day I'm in a little gourmet shop that specializes in French cheeses and dessert items. Still thinking of those Eskimo women chewing for their parents, I'm having trouble doing any worthwhile shopping. Finally, I buy Ted two pounds of brandied cherries. As long as he can't wear them on his ears, I feel certain he'll like them. Now for Martha. I look up at a shining mountain of white food processors, able to grind, purée, stir, ærate, among other verbs. I ask the clerk to wrap one and enclose this card: "When Mother needs an ice floe, remember who owns the food processor. Love, Jane."

BOP

THE MACHINE WOULD not cooperate. It photographed his original, but when Oleg looked in the metal pan, the duplicate was zebra-striped and wordless. Three more times he inserted the grocery ad. He got back stripes leaning toward each other and crossing in the middle like insane skate blades.

"Please, if you will."

It was obvious that the woman wasn't interested in her job. You could tell by the way she handled the paper. Her nails tore the pleasant green wrapping that reminded him of larger American money. Her eyes never met the machine that perhaps needed ink, fluid, straightening, or encouragement. Her behavior wouldn't be tolerated if he ran the place.

"Can I ask you something?" she said.

"It is free country. One may ask what one wishes."

"You come here every day with something different. I know I'm not supposed to look, but here you are again Xeroxing garbage and your machine is acting up. Why do you make me so busy?"

"Please, I will tell you. The duplication of materials is of great interest to me. Since I came to this country, for three years now, I make copies of everything. If I could, I would copy my hair, my clothing, my food, and my bowels."

She had walked away. He left the office carrying the perfect finished copies of the grocery ads. These went into the large books stamped *Souvenirs* purchased from Woolworth's. He had filled fourteen already.

Now he was back in his small apartment, whose attitude toward America was one of total acceptance. Plastic-molded coral and gold-flecked seats blended with torn leather. A portrait of a sailboat edged up to a Degas dancer. A Cubs schedule followed. Family photos marched along in the parade. A wall clock resembling an owl's face kept the beat. And leading the line was a caricature that a street artist had done at a fair. Since he already thought he resembled a red-haired Pinocchio, the artist didn't need to use much imagination. His eyes were blue points, his mouth a slit, his ears question marks, and his nose pointed aggressively, like a blind man's white cane. His hair was unruly. He was never going to get on a beauty pageant, but maybe his odd array of features would not be discouraged on the quiz shows he loved to watch.

"Please," he'd say to the check-out girl, "what city has the highest ratio of pets to people?" If she didn't know it was Los Angeles, he'd tell her right out. But he wouldn't embarrass her. He'd say it gently, as if he were providing her with a blessing. One check-out woman, whose badge read *Marta*, seemed especially eager to see him on market days. "There's Mr. Know-It-All," she told her bag boy. They both laughed. Americans were very pleasant.

Upstairs the jesters were at it again. That's not what they were called, but he could never remember the name for what they were. How could two men practicing the art of silence make so much noise? Was it the rope pull or the human washing machine they were doing? Were they sizzling down to the floor like angry bacon, or were they sentimental clowns on an invisible tightrope? He hated what they did. It reminded him of loneliness, of which he already had enough evidence. He had taken to tapping the ceiling with a broom lately. The jesters had taken to giving him free tickets to their performances.

He went to the kitchen, poured lukewarm tea into a *Star Wars* glass, and went back to the letter he'd left that morning.

"I am sorry to say," he continued, "that there is proliferation of bad ideas here. It reminds one, if you please, of the duplication industry. For a nickel, which is very small, a man can copy anything, including his ears. However, who is it that needs four ears? The same with ideas. Everyone in America has the opinions. I read a paper and there is opinion on where dogs should leave their excrement, there is opinion on homosexuals adopting infants, there is opinion on facial hair and robins. There is opinion on cooking cabbage without odor. A child even has opinions. He thinks the governor is fat. Here is large black cat in ad choosing one cat food. If you please, why is every goddamned thing discussed in America?"

He would leave the "goddamned" out when he sent it to the "Personal View" column of the paper. If it was printed, which it wouldn't be with cursing, he'd receive five hundred dollars. But for now it exhilarated him to curse. He pounded the table for emphasis. The red Formica was unresponsive.

He worked every night from nine until five in the morning. His job was to sit at a switchboard that was hooked into store alarms. If an alarm rang, his switchboard would wail, and he would call the police, giving them a code, and call the store owner with the news. In his eleven months of employment, there'd been only twenty-seven alarms, and most of those were due to faulty wiring. He was able to spend most of his time sleeping, just as Mr. Kaplan had suggested upon hiring him. Mr. Kaplan had been insanely happy to give him a job. Just sixty years ago, Mr. Kaplan's own father had come over here, untrained, illiterate, and if it weren't for a *landsman*, he would have perished. Mr. Kaplan got very emotional then and swiped at his eyes with a big hanky and hugged Oleg Lum stiffly and told him, "Welcome, brother." Oleg thought Kaplan might burst into an American spiritual song. Although his job paid minimum wage, he had his days free to do as he wished. Usually he wished to go to the library.

The influx of Russian immigrants to the Rogers Park area had altered its environment. Russian shoemakers hung shingles on every block. Several Russian delicatessens displayed gleaming samovars next to pickled fish in windows, and the library had begun to carry a good amount of Russian-language books but mostly the classics. He had already read those books in Russian, which he had once taught. Now he wanted to read American books rich in history: Sacco and Vanzetti, Sally Rand, Nat Turner, and Howard Hughes. And when he flashed his neat green library card at the girl, who even in summer required a sweater, she always smiled at him. Maybe she, like Mr. Kaplan, assumed he was uneducated, a pretender to the American shelves. She never spoke, but once when he'd asked for a book on the process of photocopying, she had looked worried, as if her patron might be a spy.

He liked sitting at the blond wooden tables with the other patrons. Though protocol barred speech, there was good spirit to share in silent reading. He liked watching the old men who moved their lips as they read. Maybe their false teeth read words differently, trying to trick them. And children, he noticed, read in the same way. For the last week he'd observed a girl about eleven years old who had been sitting across from him. She always used encyclopedias and took notes. She was plump and had hair that wouldn't cooperate. It deserted its braids and bristled in front like cactus. Maybe even American plants had opinions, he suddenly thought.

"Have a pen? Mine's out of ink."

"Please, for you to keep." He handed a ball-point to the girl. Americans were generous, and so he wished to practice in small ways. He kept pens and paper clips and rubber bands and note paper in his pockets for such occasions.

"Thanks," she said and began copying again.

He was rereading the part in *The Grapes of Wrath* in which the turtle slowly, slowly crosses the road. The passage is marked by adversity, he'd have told a classroom of students. At one point the turtle is intentionally hit by a sadistic driver, yet it survives. In fact, the driver speeds the turtle across the road with the force of his cruelty. Oleg had arrived in America in the same way: the crueler his government had become, the more reason he had to leave. He would write an article entitled "The Cruel Kick," as soon as he had a chance.

"What's your name?" she was asking.

"I am Oleg Lum."

"Nice to meet you, Mr. Glum. I'm Carrie Remm. Where're you from?"

The other people at the table were eyeing them. He suggested with a nod that they move outside. Taking her spiral, she followed.

"I am from Moscow," he said, once outside. "And you?"

"Chicago. I'm ten years old, and my parents are divorced. My mother always looks sad because she had an operation. Now she can't have children, but since she's divorced, I'm not sure it matters that she can't have children. I just think the operation was the last straw. Anyway, I like to get out of the house. She makes me nervous."

"Please, what means *last straw*?"

"It means *curtains, cut, that's it, I've had it*."

"And your mother is alone then all the time?"

"Oh, she calls her friends. But she never goes out. When my dad comes to pick me up on Sundays, she looks a little better."

Cars whizzed by, as Lum smoked a cigarette. He liked the bold bull's-eye of Lucky Strikes.

"You would like a cigarette?" He kept an extra pack at all times for his generosity training.

"No thanks. Kids don't smoke here."

"You would like maybe ice cream?"

They walked silently to the Thirty-One Flavors, took a corner booth, and talked all afternoon.

17

They decided on dinner for Saturday night, his night off. On Saturday night Mr. Kaplan's son Denny answered the phones for time and a half. Once when Denny had had a tooth extracted, Oleg had taken his place.

He was worried about Mrs. Remm's grief. Losing one's reproductive ability, he imagined, was tragic for a thirty-four year old woman. He might buy her a get-well card, but he didn't know that she was really ill. Maybe a sympathy card was in order, and flowers, but they'd have to wait for Saturday.

"Please, if you may help," he asked a small wizened woman who looked like a lemur he'd seen at Brookfield Zoo. When one got old, hair and face turned gray together, and fine down started growing everywhere. The woman's cheeks, chin, and ears were furry. She looked as if someone had spun a web over her.

"Yes?"

"If you please, a dozen flowers."

"We have roses, carnations, combos, mixed in-season, zinnias, peonies, Hawaiian, birds-of-paradise, honeymoon bouquets, orchids, the woodsy spray, and dried. Can you be more specific?"

"The woman has lost her reproductive abilities. I wish to supply her with flowers."

"How about roses?"

They cost him fourteen dollars and ninety-five cents, and accompanying them was a card with etched blue hands folded in prayer. Inside, the card read, "With *extreme* sympathy upon your loss." He signed it Oleg, hoping for the intimacy of first names. No one called him Oleg anymore, except an old friend from Moscow he saw now and then at The Washing Well. Sometimes it was hard to remember that Oleg was his name. "In *extreme* sympathy," he repeated, liking especially how the word *extreme* looked in italics. They were a marvelous invention. He hoped for an entire

18

evening of wavy italic emotion. When he caught his reflection in shop windows, his nose appeared optimistically upturned, and the bouquet he held, wrapped in paper depicting a trellis of ivy and roses, waved like a banner.

"Get the door," he heard through the wood after he'd been buzzed into Claire Remm's apartment-building hallway. Claire was a lovely name. It reminded him of water.

When Carrie opened the door, she appeared cross. "You're on time. I thought you were the pizza. I was hoping it'd come first."

"I am not pizza. However, it is good to be here." He hoped she wouldn't assume the flowers were for her. He hid them behind his back. Since she didn't ask what he was holding, he knew she understood.

"Mom, it's Mr. Glum."

"Who?" She sounded confused, but her voice was melodic, a song, a tribute.

"My friend, Mr. Glum."

Never, he thought, had so much natural beauty been wasted on such a negligent caretaker. Not on the American side of Niagara Falls, not in those Tennessee caves where stalagmites and stalactites are overwhelmed by tepees and imitation Indian blankets. Claire Remm had blue eyes, shiny black hair one usually saw on Japanese women, and a complexion somewhere in the range of infant pink. She wore furry slippers, blue jeans, a sweat shirt that said SPEED WAGON, and no make-up. Her hair wasn't combed but stuck over one ear as if it had been glued there. Her eyes looked dried up, like African drinking holes.

"For you, Mrs. Remm, with thanks." Oleg extended the flowers in a shaky hand.

"Who are you?" she asked, peering over the flowers. She had the look of someone who doesn't care she's being observed, a look he'd seen on sleepers and drunks.

"I am Oleg Lum, friend of Carrie."

"I thought…Well, I'm sorry, Mr. Lum. I thought Carrie had invited a child."

"It is no problem. I eat very little. Like a child." He smiled so hard he thought his face might crumble.

"You don't understand, Mr. Lum. I've ordered a pizza. I assumed you two would eat and watch TV while I read a book." Her thin neck wobbled.

"The plans can exist. And may I ask, what book is engaging you?"

"*Pride and Prejudice*. I haven't read it since college."

"Is tale of civil-rights movement or of women's movement?"

Claire laughed and called Carrie. "Why didn't you explain, Care?" Carrie shrugged her shoulders and left the room again.

He pointed the flowers in Claire's direction, and she finally took them. "Please," he said, "if problem, I can exit."

"No, Mr. Lum. The pizza should arrive soon. Would you like a beer?" She had put the flowers on a silver radiator.

"May we plant the flowers?" Oleg asked.

"Oh," she said and told Carrie to get a vase and water. Lum wasn't certain, but he thought maybe she was smiling ever so slightly like someone who is trying not to laugh at a joke.

While Carrie and Claire sat on the couch, Lum sat in an oversized tan corduroy chair that made him feel fat. He assumed that the chair was Mr. Remm's and that Mr. Remm was a large man with bristly hair like Carrie's. He wondered if it made Carrie sad that he was sitting in her father's chair. He would have asked, but Claire and Carrie were watching *Dance Fever*. They concentrated on it like scholars at the Moscow Institute of Technology.

"Is good for fashion education."

"You bet," Carrie assured him. Claire watched the television and absent-mindedly dissected the pizza, which sat in the middle of the floor. Carrie had placed the roses next to the pizza in a green vase that hid their stems. He wondered whether Claire might reach for pizza and come up with a rose. The room appeared freshly painted, meaning that everything had been taken down and the walls whitewashed. No decorations had been rehung where picture hooks and curtain rods waited. It looked as if a civilization had perished there. The place made him feel foolish. It was not the first American home he'd visited. Mrs. Kaplan's was, with its plastic-covered everything and miniature dog statues and candelabra. But hers could have been the aberration. Suppose Americans were more like Danes in character than he'd imagined: melancholic, spare, and joyless.

During a commercial he spoke. "Mrs. Remm, your daughter is very clever girl and hard worker at library. She tells me about you. She is sorry for you."

"She is?" The voice was shrill, a verbal grimace.

"She is sad that you are not able, may I say, to reproduce."

"Carrie, why did you tell him *that*?" The entire room vibrated with new energy. He imagined lamps crashing to the floor. Carrie shrugged her nonchalant shoulders.

"I am sorry, Mrs. Remm, to cause this trouble. She is loving you and wanting to be of help."

Now Claire was smiling and Carrie exhaling. It couldn't have been his explanation. Some signals, he imagined, like those third-base coaches use to coax on their runners, must have been exchanged in the blink of an eye. The blink must have been invented for such a purpose. What had happened in the invisible moment was a détente. Finally Carrie spoke. "Mom, he's okay to tell things to. Who do you think he knows?"

Lum smiled. He knew he'd been insulted, but the insult was harmless. Besides, it had made Claire smile again.

"Mr. Lum," she began, "I expected a little Russian boy. You know. Pointy ears. Fat cheeks. Shorts. Sandals. Instead, you walk in knowing everything about me, bringing me flowers. I guess I must be very glum!"

They all laughed. It was a moment of joy, one he'd recall along with his first erection and leaving Russia. A triptych of pleasure. Claire kept laughing even after he and Carrie had finished. Quacking and quacking like a beautiful blue-eyed duck until she said, "I haven't read the card. Let's read the card." She opened it with high drama and stared at Lum's hopeful smile. More signals were exchanged with Carrie, who, after reading the card aloud, stared at Lum too. Mother and daughter then slapped hands palm to palm, and Claire suggested that they all take a walk.

"Better yet," Oleg said, "a trick is up the sleeve. I have procured tickets for an event of pantomime to begin in twenty minutes. We should begin our arrival now."

Claire excused herself. He and Carrie stood in the doorway at nervous attention. He could look beyond Carrie and see down the hallway to the roses opening in the vase next to the pizza cardboard. "Let's go," Claire was saying as she joined them, "or we'll be late." She was dressed as an Indian princess.

Dear Readers of Chicago:

It strikes me as new American that much is made of large-ness in your country. Examine, if you please, the Mount Rushmore. Here are the great stone faces of the profound leaders of men. But here is a man also. He is cleaning the stone faces. Up the nostril of Abraham Lincoln, freer of slaves, the cleaner climbs, as a fly, without notice. Or, let us say, a family on vacation takes his photo. There is the great stone Lincoln. There is the tiny man with huge brush for nostril cleaning. Thus is humor because the size of man is made small by large design of beauty.

In America I hear many jokes. Some are about women whose husbands cannot meet their desires, which are too large. In others, several members of Polish nation are trying to accomplish small goal, the removing of light bulb. Their effort is too large for smallness of task.

On a certain Sunday I was driving with American acquaintance down the Madison Street. My American said, "You'll never believe what we waste our money on here," and it is true that in Soviet Union largeness is always minor premise of grandeur. There are large monuments to workers, huge squares to fill with people cheering for politics, heads of Lenin the size of cathedrals, and many women with large breasts, who are called stately by the Russian men. Now on American Sunday I look to right, and there stands a huge bat of metal. It stands, perhaps, fifty feet tall like apartment building. I say to my friend, "The baseball is grand American entertainment. The baseball is your Lenin." "No," says American friend, "the bat is joke about wasting money. It has nothing to do with baseball."

The bat is then humorous. I believe words of my friend, who is businessman. In poor or undemocratic countries there is no humorous public art. History is the only public art. The huge stone pyramids are not meant as joke. In America the bat of abundance is cynic's joke. Same cynic points at huge genitals of corpse. He makes public monument to frozen bat. The lover of art points to the living genitals or makes the beautiful statue like Michelangelo's *David*.

As the huge Gulliver was tied down by the little citizens for possible harm done, so the public shows the disdain for size, even with its power. Thus is opposite, humor from largeness. The bully is, yes, strong, but he is also fool. He is laborer digging in dirt. His brain is mushroom producing no truths. Largeness is victory and also defeat. To largeness we prostrate ourselves and then up our sleeves die laughing.

Thank you,
Oleg Lum

Since it was Sunday and Carrie would be away, he thought of calling Claire and arranging a private visit. The evening before had been a success, the pantomimists having done a version of *Antony and Cleopatra* in which the larger, bearded Cleopatra swooned into the compact Antony's arms. Carrie quacked like her mother. Claire cried when she was happy. Both mother and daughter had walked him

23

home, kissed him good night, and said they'd treat him to lunch on Monday.

If he called her now, the spell might be broken. She'd infer the obscene length of his nose in his altered phone voice. She'd laugh at his misuse of articles. He'd not flirt with ruin. The beach beckoned with its Sunday collage of summer bodies.

"What is your name, little boy?" Lum asked the child who sat next to his towel squeezing sand between his toes. He wore a seersucker sunsuit and a bulging diaper. His cheeks were fat, but he was not tan. In fact, he was pale and resembled Nikita Khrushchev with his spikes of just emerging white-blond hair. He was no older than a year and a half, though Lum might be wrong, having had no experience with babies.

"Do you know your name?" Lum asked again. The sun was behind them, and he felt his skin radiating heat. He'd fallen asleep in the afternoon, and, judging by the sun's angle, he'd slept two or three hours. It was evening. People were beginning to pack up for the day. The lifeguard, who had made a white triangle of cream on his nose, looked bored. Not enough people were swimming, Lum observed, much less drowning, to give his life definition.

Lum offered the child a piece of banana, which he greedily accepted. He mashed it in his hand and pressed pieces slowly into his mouth.

"Bop," said the boy.

"Pleased to meet you. I am Oleg Lum." The child looked at Lum's extended hand.

"Of course, babies do not understand the handshake," he explained. "Tell me, little Bop, is your mama here?"

Bop stood on tiptoe in the sand, wobbled, and tumbled to Lum's towel. A cascade of sand followed him.

Lum pointed at a young couple loading cans of Coke into a cooler. "Do you know these people, little Bop?"

24

Bop ignored all questions, sharing Lum's blanket, kicking his feet in the air, and humming, "Gee-dah, Gee-dah."

After an hour of Bop's company, Lum thought of asking the lifeguard about a lost-and-found service. He was afraid, though, that the lifeguard would call the police and scare the boy, who looked at Lum with such peaceful eyes, who joyously accepted crackers, and who laughed at the seagulls' W-shaped assaults, at bugs he found in the sand, and at Lum cooing, "little Bop, little Bop."

Bop had fallen asleep at the edge of Lum's towel, sucking the corner he held in his fist. Lum folded another triangle over his back to protect it from the waning sun.

When the lifeguard was tying up his boat and the sun had changed to a forgiving twilight, in which couples twisted together on blankets or faced each other with their legs folded Indian-style to share a joint, Lum realized there were no families left to step forward and claim Bop. It was clear in this instant that he would either have to call the authorities, men whose hands shot lead at robbers, who poked sticks into kidneys, or keep the child with him. The law would not recommend that decision, he was sure, but parents who'd forgotten a child at the beach, in the way he might leave an umbrella on a bench, weren't worthy of a search.

He'd carry the child home with him. In the morning he'd read the paper, hoping for news. And if news didn't materialize, there was Claire waiting, arms open, bereft of the ability to reproduce. She had said the night before, admiring Carrie's impressions of the mimes, that she'd have liked to have had one more child, a son. Then she'd wrinkled her nose, frowned, smiled, looked away, asked for a cigarette, and shrugged. Every emotion could be observed as it changed direction like a sailboat wobbling to shore in cross winds. She'd thank him for the child. It was clear the police weren't needed.

The lifeguard had left the beach, surrendering the safety of its inhabitants to Lum. He'd not disappoint the lifeguard.

He put his book and wallet and keys in his back pockets, slid into his sandals, gathered the child up in his towel, and began walking, Bop snoring soundly in his arms.

He'd never thought of having a child himself. He had spent his years getting out of Russia, while other men searched for lovers or wives. Now, diapering the boy with the clean supplies he had bought at midnight last night when the need presented itself, it seemed he had never done anything more natural. Lum soothed Bop's rash with Vaseline, powdered his plump half-moons, and watched in awe as Bop cooed and pulled his pink penis, doubling over it, snail-like, and curling around his softer part. At least the parents had fed the poor child and not in any way hurt him. He was mottled pink, plump, and clean in all places but the creases, which were easy to overlook even if one was diligent.

The seersucker sunsuit was drying in the washroom. The child had eaten crackers, cheese, a peach, and milk already. Bop pronounced "milk," "shoe," "dog," and "bird." Lum pronounced, "Little Bop is very clever." Bop pointed at Lum, wordless. The morning passed quickly.

Walking to Claire's, he hoped that Bop would not soil himself on Lum's new shirt. He had even given Bop a bath for the occasion and combed his sparse hair so it stood in neat little rows, like toy farm crops. He wanted to meet Claire upstairs with the child rather than on the street, where her reaction might be too private for display. Suppose she thanked him with tears or fell into his arms, a crest of emotion filling her chest. Suppose she suggested marriage on the spot, Oleg Lum the father of little Bop, she the mother, Carrie the big sister, a home on a quiet street, maybe a dog, lots of American television to cool his rapid-fire brain. He carried Bop, who mostly smiled. Lum smiled too. It might be his wedding day.

"Just a minute," he heard through the door. As he'd hoped,

Claire answered. But she didn't meet him with sobs or whispers of praise.

"What, Oleg!"

"Is boy I found at beach. Is he not handsome?"

"You found him at the beach? Didn't he have parents?"

"Parents could not be located. I wait until beach closes and only drug takers remain. Then I take him home."

"He spent the night with you? You didn't call the police?"

"I do not want government thug with stick in belt to take child and frighten him. I want you to take him."

"Me, Oleg?"

Lum looked hopeful. Bop offered Claire a sucked-on cracker.

"Oleg, let's sit down." They walked into the front room. Carrie was not home. Bop sat on the floor and busied himself by dismembering a magazine. "I know you mean well, Oleg, but laws are strict. If a child is lost, he must be given to the authorities. They'll find his parents."

"Parents dump child on beach like trash. They leave him there. Why should such parents have themselves found?"

"It's true, Oleg, but there are laws. I wouldn't be surprised if his damned Easter picture weren't being flashed on every newscast."

"Is no damned flashing. I watch last night and news today."

"Oleg," Claire continued, "you could be considered a criminal."

"Is no crime to help little Bop and to hope that you will also help."

"How do you know his name?"

"I ask him, 'Baby, what is your name?' He says, 'Bop.'"

"Oleg, Bop isn't an American name. Bop isn't any kind of name. Babies make sounds."

"Bop is not name. Parents are not caring. Police are not called. What should I do? Take baby back to beach? Leave him in rowboat like Moses?"

27

"No, Oleg. I'll call the police. They'll come for him and find his parents or relatives. You were very kind to care for him. Bop is lucky to have found you, Oleg." She kissed the crown of his head.

"Please, before police, let us sit together and watch Bop."

Claire sat down next to him, and he took her hand. Bop was pretending to water some violets with an empty watering can. Then he sat down opposite Oleg and insisted, plainly, on milk. Claire got a small glass and offered it to Bop.

"He is needing help," Oleg suggested and held the glass for him.

They sat hand in hand for an hour, Oleg enjoying the most mundane fantasy. They were at an American pediatrician's, taking their child for a checkup. She was the bride he'd met in college, and she still wore her modest wedding ring, though he'd have liked to have been more extravagant. She didn't have to talk, his wife of many years, just sit and admire their little son.

"Police are not needing to be called."

"I'll call them now, Oleg. I'll explain. You go home, and I'll phone you after they've left."

Lum felt large tears forming under his lids. He watched Bop shredding the interior-design magazine. The blurry room lost its sofa, its draperies, its rug. Everything was in pieces. This was not to be his wedding day.

Dear Personal View:
    Everything in America gets lost, sometimes stolen. I lose my umbrella on el train. It is never returned. Meanwhile, baby is left on beach to weather, danger, criminals, drug takers, God knows. Parents come to police. Say they are sorry, so baby is returned. Why in America is easier to find lost baby than umbrella costing nine dollars? But I worry most for sandy American baby who is found on beach like walking rubbish heap called Bop. He is dirty, hungry little immigrant. I give him new life visa, which police revoke.

The switchboard was howling. An alarm had gone off at Cusper Motors, but Lum closed his eyes and listened as the howling continued. He was not going to call the police. Let the thieves do as they wished to Cusper's Fords. The police were worse than criminals. They were blind men, liars, fools. Lum disconnected the phone, and in the sudden silence, he willed his eyes closed and tried to fall asleep. He would sleep until his shift ended, until all Mr. Cusper's Fords were taken, until the police were running over the whole city in search of car thieves and drug takers and lost babies.

INFINKS

IN THE SHARK-GRAY Lincoln limousine that Ben had rented for three hundred dollars, Sam and Gilsa laughed from too many joints and shared a private awe as fog plunged into the Sonoma Valley. John poured drinks for all except Sarah, who was trying to get pregnant and thought that drinking might discourage the healthy sperm from spawning with the egg upstream. Rita sat backward on a folding leather stool, watching hills and vineyards announce themselves to her after they had disappeared to the others. Sitting in this way was appropriate for her fortieth birthday, a time to look back at the fifteen years she and Ben had shared.

"Such fun," Gilsa slurred.

It wasn't her French-Swiss accent that put Rita off as much as her expertise in everything. Her accent seemed like another skill she had developed for Sam to score. Usually Rita would have signaled her annoyance to Ben, but Ben, admiring the view, the chauffeur's driving, the achievement of such surprise, was hardly a partner tonight. What Ben would do when she turned fifty had been Rita's other thought. Really, she couldn't imagine. He could already be planning something, Ben, who told her so little, who worked so hard at his obstetrics practice and barely seemed to notice it was anyone's birthday until a limousine gave proof of his involvement.

When Rita later told him that the birthday had made her uncomfortable, Ben's eyelids puckered in indignation. He blamed it on Gilsa and Sam: "There's nothing worse than stoned Republicans."

But it wasn't the evening that should have been different. It was Ben. Something had to be done about him, yet Rita wasn't sure what. She was forty, and they were childless, though Ben had wanted children for many years of their marriage. Their lives had always been going too well to risk changing them. Maybe it was turning forty itself that had created the need for action. Maybe it was the limousine ride that reminded her of funerals. Maybe it was driving backward through fifteen years of accceptable marriage and questioning her standard. Maybe it was Ben with his smug good plans.

Whatever it was caused Rita to swing into action, tying her hair back, chain-smoking, and making phone calls. She had threatened Ben with the project since the wildlife center down the road to Muir Beach had opened. Its purpose was to rehabilitate animals that had been injured by man or environment. Ben called it the broken zoo. Now Rita phoned Mrs. Bryan and said she was willing to become part of the research team. She would take the next goose that hatched and adopt it for the imprinting study.

Driving to the center, Rita felt slightly insane. Her eyes were glazed over. Her temples throbbed. She drove too quickly, worrying that the goose would arrive before she did. But, of course, there were other geese. And even yesterday she hadn't considered being part of the project. Why was it that suddenly she had to participate? If the goose were a male, she'd call it Stanley after Stanley Mosker, whom she had loved in first grade. He had a great mole on an earlobe and grass-colored feline eyes. If it were a girl, she'd call it Charlotte, which is what she had always wanted to call a daughter in the days when she had wanted children.

It was a gentle evening, the sun dipping behind trees, an almost passive breeze, very warm for May. In ten years we could all be dead, she thought, and cried big tears that hit the steering wheel.

"Get Charlotte off the table," Ben said as Rita drank her morning coffee. Charlotte was three months old now, and her downy feathers were turning stiff. Still, she seemed to Rita like an infant needing protection, even from Ben's criticisms.

"Imagine what it's like when a teacher criticizes your child," Rita said.

"You obviously don't understand that Charlotte's a genius even though she is a goose," Ben said. "I'll have the school board look into your record on equal opportunity. I bet it's not the first time a goose has been made an example in your classroom."

Charlotte sat patiently at Rita's feet. Every now and then she made a noise that was close to a honk but always a decibel too high so that it sounded more like a complaint.

"We'll have to start saving for her education," Ben said.

"You know, Ben," Rita felt obliged to say, "I didn't get this goose to replace a child. I could still bear a child if I wanted. Ellie Lawson had a perfectly healthy son last year, and she's forty-three."

"I was at the big event."

"And remember what I did before I married you?"

"You slept with your professors."

"Funny."

"You were a biologist and a Woodrow Wilson Fellow. Did you know that, Charlotte?"

Charlotte was cocking her head toward Ben. Rita was sure she knew her name, though it's always too easy to assume what an animal knows.

Sarah was five months pregnant and starting to show. Rita asked her to lunch so they could talk, which they hadn't done in several months. Rita wondered whether Sarah's being pregnant made her nervous around Rita. Everyone thinks I want to get pregnant, Rita thought. Charlotte had followed into the bathroom, where Rita was lining her eyes. She didn't understand why she felt it necessary to line her eyes for Sarah's visit, but having an almost grown goose with her in the bathroom didn't help to steady her hand. "Get out of here, Charlotte," Rita told the goose.

Today Charlotte seemed to have amnesia. She wouldn't respond to her name at all. She sat on the edge of the sink pecking at the mirror. "Get the hell out," Rita told Charlotte and pushed her to the floor. It was her first instance of goose abuse.

Sarah looked radiant as pregnant women allegedly look. Her complexion glowed, her stomach made a delicate slope under her denim jumper, and she was eager to describe every movement that her baby made in the womb.

"I've quickened, Rita. I can actually feel her move. Why did I wait this long?"

Rita supposed she wasn't expected to answer. Anyway, she didn't know. The coffee was ready, so she poured each of them a cup.

"Oh, no," Sarah protested. "It changes the fetal heart rate. It gives the baby tachycardia.'"

"Bump bump bump bump bump bump bump," Rita said to illustrate.

"What?" Sarah asked.

"Nothing. Want some megavitamins or some juice?"

"No thanks. Rita, I brought some pictures."

"Did John fashion a periscope?"

"No, there's a book from Sweden. Here's a photo of a five-month fetus. Can you imagine that it already looks like us?"

"This one looks like a loaf of bread with hair. Yours looks better, I'm sure."

Charlotte was sitting at Rita's feet. Sarah kept eyeing Charlotte suspiciously.

"Mrs. Bryan at the Center tells me that Charlotte is very intelligent. If my data is correct, she knows her name, my name, Ben's name, how to get into the bathroom when the sliding door is closed, and how to show Ben that she wants the water turned on."

Sarah didn't acknowledge her. She was looking outside Rita's window at a layer of fog covering Mt. Tamalpais. "You know, I think I got pregnant on your birthday, Rita. The fog was the same that night."

Charlotte was standing in the middle of the kitchen flapping her wings. Outside two blue jays were contesting territory, circling around and around a redwood tree.

"Want some tea or a sandwich?"

"I have to go, Rita. I'm learning to crochet this afternoon at The Knittery. The class is at one. Want to join me?"

"Thanks anyway, Sarah. Charlotte has a checkup this afternoon."

Rita knew that she was avoiding friends since her birthday and that Charlotte was a convenience. It was even a way of avoiding Ben, feigning deep involvement in her project that would end in four weeks when Charlotte would be six months old.

Now that she could fly, she was destructive around the house, and Ben decided she'd have to stay in the yard. Of course, Charlotte, with her keen sense of humor, took it out on Ben. All week she had been following him to work, trailing after his car as it headed toward San Rafael until he had to return home and lock the goose in the garage. "Imagine," Ben said, "telling your patients you're late because a goose was following you!"

In laughing, Rita burned her tongue on her coffee. She felt a little peeved that Charlotte chose to follow Ben, who hadn't even fed her or paid her any mind. And when Charlotte wasn't following Ben, her new habit was to sit in the carport waiting for him to return. Rita noted in her log that Charlotte's behavior seemed a bit neurotic since she'd been banished to the yard. Then she crossed it out. It didn't seem fair or scientifically objective to call Charlotte's interest in Rita bonding with a mother figure and her interest in Ben an obsession.

Rita decided to go for a ride. She needed some vegetables for dinner and a birthday gift for Gilsa.

To her disappointment, Charlotte didn't follow Rita's car into Mill Valley. She looked overhead several times but saw no hopeful vee in the sky. Ben had said it was odd recognizing the bird following you as you might spot an old acquaintance at an airport. Rita looked in her rearview mirror at the warm blue sky filled with nothing.

Now that the bird was gone, Rita asked Ben if he'd like to spend a weekend with her in the country. The question sounded too formal. Besides, she didn't want to spend time with Ben at all. She just wanted to get away. Thinking of herself asking in the first place, Rita felt twelve years old and dishonest, as if she were bargaining with her parents about when to leave for Four Leaf Clover Camp. She'd always make alternative plans when it was time to go. Trips to museums, libraries, visits to elderly relatives – anything to postpone her inevitable departure. Once she got there, with riding and swimming and cookouts and only a few mean girls who'd pinch her in the dressing room, she never really hated it. Rather, she dulled her personality, toned down her laugh, and peered up instead of looking directly at people. Maybe the same strategy would get her through the weekend with Ben.

On the way to Little River Inn, they didn't say much. They gossiped about Gilsa and decided that the problem with Sam and Gilsa – most problems were with couples, it seemed – was that they lacked a sense of humor. When a sense of humor surfaced, as it had the night of Rita's birthday, it was so private their friends felt they were watching a Masonic ritual. Even when Ben had suggested something very funny to add to Gilsa's achievements, Sam and Gilsa had eyed Ben like a man with food on his mustache.

"What was it you asked Gilsa?"

"I asked her if she wasn't the first woman to have scaled Mount Everest in high heels."

They laughed again at his joke. Gilsa had liked the *Cooking Hungarian* book they'd given her for her birthday. "Sicilian Grecian Vegetarian Hungarian," Sam had sung, his new mantra.

Though the inn's choice rooms away from the kitchen had been taken, their room was pretty with tiny cinnamon flowers dotting everything, like chiggers, Ben said. All Rita could picture were Charlotte's tracks in the mud of their yard. In thousands of years, when their own civilization had gone to defeat, an archæologist might find the fossil tracks and conclude that domestic geese had been part of Northern California culture. Rita was sorry to mislead the woman, whom she pictured as a female Albert Einstein, but it was reassuring to know that Charlotte's feet might get them into history. Nothing else she could imagine would remain of them.

At dinner the couples opposite them were elderly and freckled. The women had snowy hair that bristled around their heads. One man had a full head of palomino-colored hair that swirled on his forehead like the curve of a conch shell. Their dinner conversation centered on flagstone versus concrete for walkways. It was one of those conversations that might have gone unspoken. At the end of the dinner the couples' voices rose to an uncomfortable pitch, and Rita, who had been focusing on her stuffed trout as a means of avoiding Ben, was relieved to have a new point of concentration, the argument that ensued over the bill.

"Me and Helen aren't poor, goddamn it," the one with the lovely hair was saying, "but don't you know, before I can eat my pie, you always grab the bill."

The other man, bald, smaller in frame and more reserved in tone, was saying, "Calm down, Whitney." But Whitney and Helen in unison, as if on cue, had stormed out, a wind of indignation trailing them through the dining room filled with crystal, daffodil wallpaper, hanging plants, and cut wildflowers.

"That's what I like about vacations," Ben said. "They bring out the best in people. I've noticed, Rita, that this vacation has made you particularly talkative."

"I guess I haven't much to say."

"Empty-nest syndrome."

"No, it's turning forty."

"You seem to have forgotten that we're the same age, that you, in fact, followed me over the hill by more than six months."

"What's it like for you?" She'd never considered that he might be feeling as bad as she felt. Looking at him now, sanely for the first time in months, she did seem to detect signs of wear. His hair was longer than he usually let it go, his forehead wrinkle appeared ironed in, and his eyes looked pink and sad. She wanted to say something like "Poor Ben," but he hadn't answered yet.

"Not so bad for me," he sighed. "Thirty was bad. Remember? I kept thinking I was an adult, but I kept feeling like an adolescent with a receding hairline. Forty seems what I should be."

She felt Ben's leg touch hers under the table. "When I was thirty-five," Rita began, dropping her fork for emphasis, "I used to think, 'My life is half over.' Marking the middle seemed so neat. Now all I think is that my life is more than half over, and what have I done?"

Of course, there was nothing to say. Both knew what they had and hadn't done.

"We're still kids," Ben smiled. "Infinks." Now both his legs were touching hers.

"I was thinking," Rita said. "Maybe it isn't too late to

37

really change things. Maybe we could start again. I remember when I used to start again every year. School was about to begin, and I'd go buy my new supplies. I'd buy folders of every color and pencils to match and pens and new chewy erasers and wide-lined notebook paper and then, last, the best of all, I'd get new shoes. The soles were always beige and cleanly stitched in white. And do you know what I'd do with those shoes the first night?"

"Don't tell me," Ben teased.

"I'd sleep with them in my bed. Then school would begin, and the shoes would give me blisters. I'd have to rest them for a few days. That was my new start. Guaranteed every year. Then the day when it became fall — not the date but the weather. The air felt different, and I felt definitely older."

"That's when older was older."

"So, I was thinking," Rita continued, "we might make a new start."

"Buy some new, ill-fitting shoes?"

"No," Rita said and waited for Ben to speak. It was like waiting for the wheel of fortune to spin. If Ben suggested a baby or divorce, she'd say yes. Becoming religious, marriage counseling, and hang-gliding were definite nos. She couldn't imagine what would rate a maybe. She was too old for maybes.

Whitney and Helen returned to the dining room without their perpetual hosts. They sat across from each other and ordered second, legitimate desserts to replace the contested ones.

Ben smiled at them. It was obvious he had no suggestions for a new start.

Back in Mill Valley, Rita called Sarah. She didn't want Sarah to think that Rita wasn't interested in her pregnancy, though she wasn't. Sarah said she was big as a Winnebago and had developed varicosities. Rita offered her sympathies, which Sarah accepted, and wondered why her meager little sympathies were suitable for so many occasions. Was she ever really more sorry sometimes than others?

Then she called Mrs. Bryan to ask for a new goose to imprint.

"The imprinting project is over, honey," Mrs. Bryan said. "Besides, I've found that second geese just don't measure up."

THAT SUMMER

THAT SUMMER ALL Amy could picture were drowning
men, men drowning. On postcards they appeared, small
and hopeless on the horizon. In museum catalogues the
hulls of ships filled with them, and, God, all the awful
poems she noticed about drowning men compared to with-
ering jade plants, to fingers, to paper. No, there couldn't be
so much drowning. It must be something else, maybe bad
art, maybe the end of civilization. Amy wasn't sure.

That summer there was Raymond, who prided himself
on living through the darkest hours in his own history. Raymond of private schools for disturbed adolescents, of washroom wastebasket fires. Raymond of the insect eyes that
never closed, who loved to dance and call celebrities by
their first names. On a *Saturday Night Live* rerun, John Be-
lushi imitated Joe Cocker, rocking spastically like a fat
wind-up child, self-indulgent, sneering as beer poured out
of his mouth, wetting his shoulder. "You fucked up, John,"
Raymond said. Of course, John didn't answer. When Amy
said, "Turn it off. I don't want to see a dead man imitating
a living man," Raymond thought it too funny, laughed until
his knees ached and his eyes finally closed. Famous among
his friends for never blinking, Raymond washed out to sea,
Amy explained on her better days.

The Sunday afternoon Raymond drowned, Amy had a
cold. They were supposed to go to the lake for a beginning-
of-the-summer picnic. Amy was an art major, fond of small,
busy prints on luxurious fabrics. She would design bed-
spreads and sheets someday, she told her father's friends,

corporate lawyers, who thought Amy so lovely that they really cared what she said about raw silk. Amy's mother was usually away, a career woman before the fashion, radio-advertising trouble-shooter, jetting between Omaha and Akron, charting slumps and trends in bold red marker. When Amy was little, she'd take the marker and draw intricate maps of imaginary neighborhoods, naming them Red Rod Village and Triangle Square. Humor appeared in Amy's colorful designs, and Amy was sure it was humor that attracted her to Raymond. Tall, sweaty, uncompromising, Raymond was considered by others a pain and a tease and a bully. Still, he was brilliant, a fellowship student, the son of a Nobel Prize winner. So what if his father had lobbied for the prize, calling Stockholm as often as others call the weather? Still, Dr. Ricks had found a cure for a rare enzyme deficiency with four names.

Amy remembered a night at an art opening. The show contained erotic ceramic mugs, molded into breasts and penises and testicles and vaginas. Raymond spent the evening pretending to appreciate the work by holding it in a subtly suggestive manner. That was the charm of Raymond, Amy thought. Though he was most certainly caressing the breasts of a mug, one couldn't be certain. Raymond was the lewdest man she'd ever dated, but half the time she imagined he couldn't be doing what he plainly was. Raymond became Amy's own worst idea of men, blended with the suspicion of his innocence. "You're irony embodied," Amy told him at another picnic in front of his English-major friends, who could appreciate the comment. Raymond quickly mimed a scene from *Œdipus Rex*, of course the one in which Œdipus puts out his eyes. The picnic dissolved into hoots and laughter, since Raymond's prominent eyes would not cooperate. Even closed, playing the blinded king, they animated his face.

Amy had all the symptoms of a classic summer cold, plus a terrible taste in her mouth, as if she'd eaten some green acrylic paint, she told her mother, who smiled without looking at her. She called Raymond to tell him that she couldn't go to the picnic but to wish all of his fellow Joyce scholars well. She liked her role in the group as the nonverbal artist. It kept the pressure off. Once Lois, a stalky Ph.D. candidate, finishing her dissertation on point of view in Hardy, remarked that Amy's eyes looked subterranean, opaque, absent. Lois was a master of the triple entendre, and Amy hadn't known what to reply. "Thank you" had been her decision, and so the subject was dropped.

"I'm sick, Ray," Amy told him on the phone.

"Shit," Ray said. "And I had a surprise for you."

"Can it wait?" Amy asked.

"Not really. It's a demonstration. Remember last summer when I couldn't swim?"

The picnic last summer had been a disaster. Not only did Raymond not know how to swim, but the others, by force of Raymond's neurotic, childlike pleas not to leave him on the shore rotting like a piece of driftwood, were constrained from swimming. By the end of the afternoon, everyone was sick of Raymond, vowing to forget his phone number. Only Amy had felt sorry for him. She remembered times when she was little and her mother was away. She had interesting plans made for her in advance and money to spend on movies or ice cream. Listless, she'd sit on her bed, counting the spots on the butterflies' wings of her wallpaper or half-sleeping day and night. How can you move when you're all alone with no one to notice that you're moving? Amy loved Raymond because he couldn't bear to be alone either, would never leave her, was perfectly needy, and understood the threat of total, endless separation. Amy would lie in her bed as a child imagining the most terrible deaths for her mother. "Because you hate her for leaving you so often," a therapist once told her. "Because people die and children are left motherless," she countered in her clear, eight-year-old mind.

42

So now Raymond could swim, but no one would really care. Amy wished she felt better. "Ray?" she asked. "Why don't you come over instead? We can watch TV or sit in the yard or see my father's slides of Tahiti." It didn't sound like much fun to her either.

"Gee, uh, thanks anyway," he teased. "I'll see you this evening then."

"Okay," Amy said meekly. "I have some letters to write," though she knew they wouldn't get written. "See you tonight, and remember," she added, "to close your eyes when you swim." She pictured Raymond torpedoing through the water, open eyed, not having the sense to know that water is dirty. Amy sometimes exaggerated his lack of sense. She realized that she mothered him in contrast to her own mother's lack of involvement, and usually Raymond didn't object. Only once he had angrily said, "Until I met you, I never remembered to zip my pants. Thanks for keeping me out of the halfway house."

"Iron lungs," Amy thought. She was lying on her floor listening to the Plantagenets. The record cover showed four men dressed like royalty from the neck up with ruffles, pointy beards, and crowns. From the shoulders down they were punk. "Death," Amy thought and pictured Ann Boleyn's wardrobe, an exhibit she had admired once in England. She had seen the silk, three centuries old, and the intricate, woven fastenings. Amy hated zippers as much as she hated Raymond teasing her. Raymond had told her of a fourth-grade teacher who loved to embarrass him. Once she'd screamed, "You ran my nylon!" when he approached to show her a drawing. Another time, when he had stomach flu and needed permission to use the washroom, Miss Burch had shrieked, "You could have thrown up on me!" She was probably frigid, Amy had explained in bed with Raymond. Amy loved long summers home from college when her parents were away and she had the luxury of making love in

43

her own, comfortable bed in her room with the worn, irrelevant wallpaper. She could live without food, she thought, but summers in her parents' house were necessary. Sometimes she hoped that she, an only child, would inherit the house, where she'd never change anything and use her room for decades of love. The Plantagenets were singing, "I'm slip-slip-slipping into the abyss-byss-byss." Downstairs she could hear the insect throb of a lawn mower. Her mother was asleep in another bedroom, resting on a stopover from travel. Tomorrow she was to "problem-solve" for a Latino rock station in San Antonio.

Once when Amy was eight, she'd gone with her mother on a business trip to New York. Her father had the mumps, caught from Amy, a situation that her mother had found incredibly funny. While her mother made her rounds of stations, Amy spent her time with a droll baby sitter provided by the hotel, a premed student named Gretta, who left her textbooks on a table with lion-claw legs. First the claws interested Amy, but as the week wore on, the medical texts became her entertainment. Amy read about iron lungs and saw skin diseases in such vibrant colors that they burst before her eyes like Disney fireworks. When her mother got her home, there were long weeks of seeing Dr. Pimm, a cherubic British psychiatrist trained in treating children. No one seemed to believe that Amy's vivid nightmares were inspired by the medical texts. It had to be more, and her mother, good businesswoman that she was, was determined to find the real cause. Twice a week Amy spoke to Dr. Pimm, cautiously accepted a cup of tea with cream, and staged listless dramas with his nondescript puppets. Finally, bored by Amy's lack of progress, her mother terminated the relationship. Then her mother cut down on her amount of traveling, her father finally taught her how to ride her bike, and a new era of family harmony was launched with a trip to Disneyland. Amy remembered sitting in a little car shaped like a teacup that suddenly spun into a tunnel, cracking her front tooth. The broken tooth ended the era. School began again, and Amy went dully back, while her mother reactivated her full schedule and her father spent most of his time at the office. As Amy circled the block on her red Super-Tube bicycle, she felt vaguely grateful to Dr. Pimm.

Amy thought of Raymond's naked body, his muscular legs. She always pictured him standing. To imagine him horizontal, suspended in water, was impossible. Raymond was so quick and energized. He snapped through rooms and changed the air behind him. He danced like a dynamo. He was Amy's way of releasing herself, being real, she thought. The record was still playing, "x is not y, no, y is not x." True, Amy thought, but not very interesting. She closed her eyes but found that she couldn't breathe with one pillow. She rearranged the bed, propped herself four pillows high, and tried to sleep. This fall would be her last semester in college. She was to spend the summer testing prints that she would transfer onto cloth in the cold art studio smelling of sawdust. She pictured swirling colors, holiday reds and greens, cool blues melting into gray, swimming colors, some dangerous, others light as a glance. She traveled down long corridors of designs so intricate that she'd never be able to print them. Once she'd seen a movie in which a dying woman meets all her friends down a deep, tunneling hallway. When Amy died, she wouldn't see people, though Raymond might be there, a voice, a laugh, an amorphous good mood. Mainly there'd be colors and designs so intricate she'd never get them right, never fuse them: y is not y, but purple can dissolve into blue and red or lose its shyness and burst into fire. Amy felt herself falling asleep through the colors and the lawn mower and her mother's rousing Beethoven (always the *Eroica*).

It was about three o'clock when Raymond entered the water. He'd had half a bottle of Chianti and smoked some really good grass. "Eye-closing dope," he had called it. It felt good to be in the water. It felt endless. He closed his eyes and relaxed. He surfaced and reopened them. Why had he waited until he was twenty-three to learn to swim? Why hadn't someone told him how cold water felt, how much distance he could cover? His father wanted him to be well-rounded, a swimmer, a man. After all, hadn't he, a first-generation American, won a Nobel Prize? Couldn't he, jaw jutting, shoot a round of gold in the eighties? Raymond felt the sun pour on his head. Swimming was like an amusement-park ride. You wanted to shout. You wanted people to know you loved it. You never wanted to get out. Raymond thought of Amy, how she'd have waved to him from her Indian blanket or curled over his back like Esther Williams as he propelled them through the water. He thought of her parents, so deadly proper and aching for something. Amy's dad had actually said to him, "We think you're very liberating for Amy." He had smiled like a Boy Scout with a badge in psychology.

Now the afternoon was dimming, the wind had changed, and the skyline was dropping. The Hancock building was shrouded in clouds or smoke or fog, and cinematic blue people were gesturing from shore, past him, he thought. He had swum out too far, could never get back, he realized, and the water was feeling cold, like the air in a tent he once shared with his brother in the North Woods. His father hated camping but felt it was good for his sons. *Nature*, his father had said with too much emotion, is our *source*. His father must know about nature, Raymond conceded. So far out it was easier to feel objective, forgiving. It was like being in a plane so distant from earth that you feel compassion for people, so small, so diminished, whole cities the size of auditoriums, invisible houses, the idea of dinner tables, of couples in bed, of books open on nightstands. Now he was shaking, his legs had disappeared, his head was filling with sounds, with nothing really helpful. "Swim" or "kick" or "dummy," he kept saying but couldn't obey, and all he could see was water, and it really didn't matter. It didn't feel so bad. His arms were missing now, and all that was left was a heart, a heart in the water beating so abstractly that it wasn't Raymond.

At five the phone rang. Amy stirred, sat straight up, blew her nose and felt her forehead, probably a fever. "Mom?" Amy called. "Mom?" But instead of her mother, her father came in the room looking grave and distracted, like a bad boy sent to the principal's office. He was still wearing his mowing clothes, old shiny pants, a pink golf shirt, and the work boots that were usually banished to the downstairs utility room. So Mother was softening in her old age, abandoning rules. Amy thought it odd that a woman who logged hundreds of thousands of air miles a year could care so much about seven hundred square feet of beige carpet.

Her father was saying, "Amy, Amy." And instantly Amy knew something was wrong. Once she'd heard that tone when Aunt Emily had her first stroke, mild Aunt Emily, who'd brought Amy miniature cuckoo clocks from Switzerland and the sweetest, darkest chocolate on earth. Amy noticed her mother standing in her bedroom doorway, looking small and crumpled, like Mrs. Robinson in *The Graduate* after Benjamin takes up with Elaine. "Amy," her father said again, and Amy felt a chunk of wood in her mouth so real she could chew it. And her mother was crying and urging her father on: "Tell her, Frank. Please, Frank." And Amy seemed to miss all the connections but heard "Raymond" and "swimming" and "sorry" and "tragic." She saw her wallpaper raining and streaking. And her own hands were beige, and her fingers were gray, and maybe, she thought, she was dying, though her parents told her she had just fainted, a normal reaction to grief.

At the funeral, which Amy was too upset to attend, friends said that Raymond's father delivered a eulogy. "Raymond loved nature," he said sincerely, and people had wept. And Lois, the Hardy scholar, read something about the maiden voyage of the *Titanic*, very gripping and gray and inappropriate, Amy's father reported. Amy received polite calls from many of Raymond's friends. No one knew what to say, and Amy was unable to connect much of what was spoken.

That fall, designing the pattern for her senior project, a design so subtle it depended on texture, not color — so different, her professor remarked, from her less mature work — words came back to her. In the uncertain light of early November afternoons while Amy worked alone in the studio, words spoken to her came back, unencumbered by feeling, trees in a forest falling and only Amy to hear them.

PHANTOM PLEASURE

LACEY DAVIS LOST his right leg up to the thigh one week after he was shot by his male lover. A Saturday night, he was lying alone in bed, watching the paint on the ceiling, listening to "Party Doll" on the tape recorder. The bullet fractured the femur in three places, and the wound congealed until four the next afternoon when his mother, Floris Davis, a lifelong cleaning lady, went to locate him. It was their custom to meet at quarter to ten at the Gethsemane Baptist Church, and this was the first time Lacey had missed in seven years. Floris Davis, wearing her favorite pink hat with silver sequins, found him unconscious in bed.

"Lacey was always a good boy," Floris told Harriet Groman when she came to clean her residence for the sixteen hundred and third time in thirty-two years.

"Of course he's a good boy."

"To think. He didn't get shot up in Vietnam but in his very own bed by a bus-i-ness as-soc-i-ate." Floris stretched out the sound of the two words to conceal even from herself the nature of Lacey's attachment to Otis Balthazar.

"You're not even safe at home," Harriet said, looking at the bolted kitchen lock. "I remember when Lacey and Susan would play in our back yard. He'd run around her like a rooster, and Susan would laugh and laugh. The little drooler couldn't even keep herself sitting up."

"Well, his running days is over. He says it hurts so, even though his leg is gone. And sometimes it feels like someone's tickling his toes with a big old feather."

"Phantom pain." Harriet lit a cigarette with the one she'd smoked down to the lipstick. "They say a woman feels it when she loses a breast."

"I can believe that," Floris added, hand over her heart.

"When Lacey's feeling stronger, Susan and I will visit him. I'll mention it to her today. How would Lacey like that?"

Floris didn't answer. She watched a grease spot on the salmon-colored counter grow smaller and smaller under her ammonified rag.

Harriet stood in front of the bathroom medicine cabinet, dropped her checkered housecoat to her waist, and palpated her right breast. Although she was sixty-four, the face in the mirror hadn't caught up. The breasts were large and round and still ribbon-pink around the nipples, promising more life. Breast palpation was a weekly ritual. It kept them safe, the way taking out a million dollars in flight insurance keeps the plane righted in the neutral sky. Now the left one. She thought of Lacey groaning in his hospital bed in the orthopedic ward, but with his twelve-year-old face. It had been twenty years since Floris had brought him along on a cleaning day. Harriet could hear Floris spraying and scrubbing, spraying and scrubbing in the kitchen, one door away. She ran her palm over her still-tight neck, an area of pride. Let the waist, stomach, behind, and legs surrender to sixty-four years of use, but spare the elegant head, neck, and breasts. Fifty-fifty. A fair deal she had struck with time.

When Elizabeth saw her grandma, Harriet Groman, approach the dignified steps of the Art Institute, she yelled to her, "Grandma, Grandma, will you buy me something?" The answer was obvious, the routine a joke that Elizabeth made of her four-year-old greed.

Susan, mugging for her mother's benefit, put her hand

over Elizabeth's mouth. Shrill infant squeals leaked between her fingers. "Cool it, Elizabeth. You don't want to scare Grandma away."

Harriet lowered herself to Elizabeth's height. She respected the child's self-indulgence. "Of course Elizabeth can have a gift today."

"Oh, thank you!" Elizabeth sashayed the length of the step and back in an appreciative dance.

"Want to eat first?" Susan asked.

Harriet, engrossed in Elizabeth, remembered Susan was also there and said, "I'll have to tell you about Lacey Davis. Remember him?"

"Of course," Susan exclaimed, knowing from Harriet's way of mentioning him that the news was probably terrible. "What happened?"

Past the Chagall windows the deep-blue color of gumballs, past the student exhibit in its hopeful symmetry, they made their way, Susan pressing for one more hint, Harriet silent as the ancient Indian burial masks lining the wall to the right. Elizabeth ran ahead, listing what she'd eat for lunch: "Coke and hamburger and maybe pie. Or maybe chicken. Do they have pancakes?"

Through the cafeteria line of art students expounding on technique, businessmen greeting their lovers, and old women carefully choosing one bran muffin, Susan asked for more: "Is Lacey alive?"

"Of course."

"Is he injured?"

"I'm afraid."

"Is he hospitalized?"

"Yes."

"Mommy, can I play too?" Elizabeth asked, approving of their game.

"Was he in an accident?"

"Please, Susan, when we sit down."

Elizabeth found them a table by the window that looked out on a sculpture garden that in the summer was also an outdoor café. Rain beaded on the satyrs and gnomes and the phœnix rising out of its heap of cement. Elizabeth gazed at the statues, her face pressed to the glass, a human gargoyle.

"Well?"

"Lacey was shot in bed."

"Oh no. By?"

"A business associate." Harriet pronounced the words with the same significance Floris had given them that morning.

"Where?"

"In bed, Susan. Listen!"

"I mean, where was he injured?"

"In the thigh. He lost his leg."

"Oh no." Susan looked down, thinking of Lacey's baseball spikes the last time she'd seen him. His face receded in her memory as she tried to grab on to it.

"Floris says the missing leg tickles like it's there."

"Phantom pleasure," Susan muttered, watching Elizabeth's distorted reflection in the glass.

"I told Floris we'd visit Lacey when he's feeling better."

Susan snapped alert. "Mother, why did you do *that*?"

"Maybe we can cheer him up. Remember how well you two got along?"

"That was twenty years ago, for heaven's sake. What could I say now to make a bricklayer who just lost a leg cheer up?"

"Maybe you can bring him a book or one of your little sketches."

"I can see it now. 'Oh, thank you for *The Alexandria Quartet*. Durrell has always been one of my favorites. And the lithograph is exquisite. I'll hang it over my étagère as soon as I'm home.' Mother, are you crazy?"

"I was just trying to be nice."

"Nice is nice. Crazy is crazy."

Harriet chose not to answer. She looked as if she was staring into a private cave.

As they walked through the galleries, Susan walked ahead, thinking of little Lacey and Floris and Elizabeth, who held Harriet's hand tightly. By a Matisse portrait of a woman, Susan heard Harriet telling Elizabeth that she'd like her hairdresser to do her hair that way.

"Maybe you can bring him here and show him what you mean," Susan said, hoping to break the ice.

No reply.

"See what happens if you don't eat?" Harriet warned Elizabeth, standing in the shadow of a Giacometti. Elizabeth looked penitent. Susan rolled her eyes toward Harriet, who looked down.

On the way out, Harriet bought Elizabeth a Japanese fan in the shape of a seashell. Then they stood at the same corner, waiting for different buses to take them in similar directions, separated by two parallel blocks, enough to enforce the silence for a week. Harriet's bus approached first. Elizabeth waved frantically with her fan, blowing her blond bangs perpendicular to her forehead.

"Why not ask Floris if Lacey needs anything? Maybe we can send him a get-well gift," Susan suggested as the bus closed its doors in front of Harriet's glum mask.

Susan and Elizabeth boarded their bus and sat down next to an elderly black woman carrying two bakery shopping bags loaded with newspapers, shoes, and a head of lettuce. As Elizabeth sang an improvised song about the Art Institute and fanned the air rhythmically, Susan stared out, thinking about what would happen to Lacey, knowing it would be Floris who would have to care for her grown son. "Poor Lacey," Susan thought, feeling sorry for herself.

In the orthopedic ward of the hospital just two blocks east of where Susan's bus was stopping, Lacey Davis propped himself up on his elbows, pulled his hospital gown down over his tightly wrapped stump, took a sip of orangeade, flashed a jack of hearts, and smiled broadly.

"Blackjack!" he shouted to Otis Balthazar, who sat nauseous and shaking at his bedside.

DEGAN DYING

SINCE THE FIRE that burned down Degan's Discount Warehouse in 1968, Arthur Degan had worked at Chairs Unlimited, where plexiglass light fixtures highlighted matching plexiglass chairs designed with contortionists in mind. In the next room were the director's chairs, waiting to be matched with Hollywood magnates or widows who needed some color for their high-rise balconies. Finally there was Loungeland, Degan's favorite room, where loungers promised to twist, swirl, rock, massage, bump, and grind, he liked telling potbellied buyers' wives. And to the newlyweds starting to furnish their thin-walled apartments, Arthur Degan always asked the same question: "What do lovers need with chairs?"

He sat in the living room in his own lounge chair, inherited in 1947 when Fanny's mother died, leaving them the Valencia flatware, now owned by Lill, and a reproduction of *Song of the Lark*, lost on a moving van somewhere. Chairs Unlimited didn't sell leather. That was its one limit. Doing his best Henny Youngman, Degan said, "Please, take my life," to Lill, who refused on principle to laugh.

"Enough, Dad."

"Enough Dad to go around!"

"Really, if you can't feel your arm, you need to see a doctor."

It was true that he couldn't feel his arm. He had awakened that way, showered, hoping it would come back, called Lill, still waiting for the pins and needles of new blood, and then called work. "Watch, as soon as I hang up, I'll be like new," he told Morry Grassler. "Lill," he said, "if I can't feel my arm, how will the doctor feel it?"

"Dad, listen. You may have had a little stroke." Her hair-do made her face look asymmetrical, and Degan wondered if she might have had a stroke instead.

"Lill, what will the doctors do? Tell me I'm dying? When you're dead, you can't feel a thing. I can feel everything but my arm." He saw the sun coming through the window and landing on an end table stacked with dishes. He really should dust. He lived like a pig.

"An arm is enough not to feel, Dad." She made a loud sucking sound as if she needed to reinflate to continue. "You must want to die."

"Nuts, Lill. Besides, if I wanted to die, why would I have waited this long? You've given me plenty of opportunities over the years. Like — "

"Don't start on Franklin again. I don't want to hear." She looked down at her jogging shoes and then flashed Degan the same violated look he had seen on her face for forty-seven years. "Don't remind me of that lousy two-timer."

"Should I remind you about Teddy?" Teddy, her son, had dropped out of college and become a cocaine smuggler and a charter member of Omnivores for a Healthy Planet.

"I'm not responsible for him. Dr. Ripon says it's not my fault. If Lou hadn't died — "

"He'd be sitting here nagging me too. Lou saw a doctor, didn't he? And as for Teddy, where is he? Flying into O'Hare with a balloon of white powder stuffed up his ass? Or running around the country defending meat and potatoes against their detractors? You know what we used to call kids like him in the old neighborhood? Icemen."

"Why?"

"Because they'd end up cold and dead before too long." He was sorry that he had hurt her. She squinted and popped her lower lip in and out of her mouth like a piece of soft candy.

"Dad, you need to see a doctor. Will you come with me in the car, or do I have to call you an ambulance?"

"I've been called worse." Again she didn't laugh. "I use my best material on you, but do I even get a smile? Smiles cost so much?"

"Dad!" He knew her business voice. She'd take no more.

"Okay, I'll see a doctor, but first let's go out to breakfast. The crap they give you at hospitals could choke a goat."

He dropped his fork three times, spilled orange juice in a sticky circle on the tablecloth, and took twenty-five minutes to cut up his omelet and butter his toast. All the while, he flirted with the waitress, whom he called "sugar," though *Janice* was plainly monogrammed on her frilly pink apron. Finally annoyed at him, she said, "My name is Janice."

"Sorry, but I don't hear so well anymore, sugar. What did you say?" He winked.

After finishing his eggs, with Lill on her fourth cup of coffee, he said, "Let's go. My leg is feeling strange now too. Maybe I'm turning into one of those new chairs. Have you seen them? There's no back. It's just a seat and a bar for resting your knees. It looks like you're always praying or practicing a position in one of those love books."

It was a humid early-fall day, a day that could also have been at the end of spring. Seasons were interchangeable with him, as were funerals. Most seemed to take place in the winter, though perhaps it was the cold that made him remember those better. Lou had died on ground-hog day. Teddy had been in a play at school that morning.

A wind blew off the lake, and the air had the pungent, salty odor of a body after love. Why did Lake Michigan smell salty? Oceans he could understand. And why were there so many cars on the Outer Drive heading in their direction? Degan saw Lill sweat with the concentration this driving required. She overtook cars going the speed limit, flashed her finger at an old woman whose Cadillac lurched toward their lane. "Where's the fire?" he asked.

"Can you walk, Dad?" They had pulled up opposite the emergency-room doors, two portholed aluminum reflectors that twisted Lill's blue Vega in the middle.

"Is the Pope Catholic?" he asked, opening the car door with fumbling and curses. He plunged onto the driveway.

Three days later, as abruptly as he had collapsed, Degan woke up. His chest was attached to a machine, his mouth was taped to a tube. One eye was taped shut, and even his armpits felt wired. He was sure his toes were in sockets, and his sad old prick plugged in somewhere too. His leg and arm weren't with him. Maybe he'd left them in Lill's car. He'd ask her as soon as he could.

"Mr. Degan?" a voice in the right corner of his room said. He could hear only in that corner, and he could see only that half of the room. "How are you today, Mr. Degan?" Degan pulled off every wire and pipe he could reach with his good right arm and said, "Eat-shit-stupid-stinking-ignorant-pissbag!"

At Degan's right some daisies were propped on a table next to a kidney-shaped bowl and a plastic water pitcher. On his left could have been a nightclub with strippers, for all he knew. He couldn't move his neck or see to the left. Fanny had died in a room like this with a crazy roommate, who, as Fanny was dying, kept crying, "Lord! Lord!" He'd have Lill take him home today. Degan saw another white uniform step into his field of vision. The man was dark and had a mustache that grew over his lip.

"I hear we've arisen," the mustache said. "My name is Dr. Ravishani. I have been tending you. You have had a vascular incident, but you'll soon be propped up, and we'll make sure you find solace if you just yield and do not remonstrate."

"Eat-shit-you-stupid-catgut-pissbag!" Degan shouted, but Ravishani continued undaunted.

"I know you are hindered, Mr. Degan. It's natural to feel unused. Furthermore, I assure you we will retract your demonstratives, if you note."

In walked Lill and behind her, sheepishly plodding like a large dog on a short leash, Teddy. "Dad," she said and bent closer to kiss his good side. "They just called and said you were awake. And look who's here to see you."

"The iceman cometh."

"We're so glad you can speak, Dad. There was some worry about your speech."

"Oh?" It sounded to him as if Lill were talking to a person on the left side of the room. He wanted to be interested in what she said, but he really didn't care. And Teddy looked lost to him, like a man in a lingerie store. "Speech is fine." He made sense, but his voice sounded bumpy to him, as if someone were pounding him on the back as he spoke. "My doctor, though. Did he fall on his head?"

Teddy laughed, and Lill elbowed him.

"He's Indian, Grandpa."

"Apache?"

"From India, Dad. He speaks British English."

"He speaks Venus English."

Teddy laughed. "You know, Grandpa, it's a shame that you're sick, but it'll be really nice getting to know you better."

Degan closed his good eye and decided not to open it again until they left.

Dr. Quincy, medical examiner, was shouting out of the television about honesty. "How can you be so blind?" he was screaming at the top of his lungs. The woman he was screaming at looked menacing. Her eyebrows were angular, her eyes mean slits.

"She did it. Whatever it was, she did it," Degan said to Teddy, who dozed at his bedside. Teddy's whole body lurched forward.

"Morning, Grandpa. How are you feeling?"

"Where's Lill?"

"Oh, she had to show a house, and then she's going bowling. You know, she's the third-best bowler in her league. She averages a hundred and fifty-two."

"Splendid."

"That doctor was in before, Grandpa. He said, 'The man is soundless for strength renovation.' He's really strange."

"You know how many times I've been sick?" Degan held three fingers right in front of Teddy's nose, as if it were a vision test.

"Three?"

"That's right. One with appendix, one with gallbladder, now this. Seventy-seven years. Three times."

"Weren't you hurt in the war too, Grandpa?"

"Balls blown off." Teddy gasped. "Just kidding. A broken wrist. I tripped over a helmet on a beach in Italy. Ever been to Italy?"

"No."

"Been anywhere?"

"To Central America a few times."

"Your business. That's right. Most of the stuff comes from Colombia, I hear. I saw a whole report about how smugglers swallow balloons of the stuff to get into the country. They're called human suitcases. Only, if the balloon breaks —" and Degan gestured a cutting motion toward Teddy's neck.

"It's just like Prohibition, Grandpa. As soon as the government legalizes the stuff, there'll be no problem. And don't worry about the human-suitcase stuff. All I do is carry money back and forth. It's like I'm a banker."

"If Quincy is so smart all the time, why is he going off the air?" Degan said.

"Ratings, I guess."

"I guess." Degan closed his eye and hoped Teddy would go away. Teddy annoyed him with his good will. "I'm feeling tired," Degan said. "Don't you have some drugs to deal?"

"Mom wants me to stay with you. I told her I would till she comes back."

"Bring me two things when she comes back: the green photo album on my kitchen table and some of that stuff you sell to children."

"I don't think I should bring it here, Grandpa. It wouldn't be good for you. It has a tendency of raising the blood pressure."

"I don't want to use it. I want to call the police and turn you in, you lousy dope peddler."

A nurse brought Degan a dish of gray pudding.

"What's that? Horse brains?"

"A healthy mix of meat and vegetables."

"Feed it to my grandson. He's an omnivore." He pointed toward the door where Lill and Teddy stood. Degan could play tricks with his good eye. He could wink them in and out of view. It was the only way he could make them disappear. "I don't eat horse," he said to the nurse. She left it on the stand and said something to Lill.

Lill bent down and kissed him. "Teddy has the album, Dad. Do you want to look at it? Watch some TV? Listen to the radio?" Degan sighed, wondering if Fanny hated him all the months she was in the hospital. The disease was eating her alive, but she was always polite and cheerful. Even lapsing into a coma, she had excused herself. She must have been lying through her teeth.

"Do me a favor, Lill."

"What, Dad?"

"Come back tomorrow."

That night he removed the tape over his left eye. It let in

more dark though he'd turned on the light. Then he decided he'd kill himself before morning. Hedda Vincent down the block had done it with blue pills. The problem was that he couldn't imagine what he could use. If he ate the flowers, Lill would just laugh, and he couldn't locate anything else that had potential. Maybe he could smother himself under the pillow, but he knew for a fact, from reading somewhere, probably *Reader's Digest*, that it was impossible to make yourself stop breathing. He was no swami. "Shitting son of a bitch!" he moaned into his pillow and turned on the radio. Someone had kindly left it on a Muzak station, thinking it an old man's obvious listening pleasure. The rendition of "Misty" sounded like raindrops beating a xylophone to death. He tried turning the dial, but he found he couldn't move his body well enough to reach the selector. He batted at the radio with his fist until it hung on its cord, swinging near the floor. The album was on his bed within reach. There was little Degan, propped against a piece of fur, dressed in a bonnet and those little potato-sack dresses that boys wore in 1907. There was his mother, corseted, standing near a huge fern. Her eyes were kind. Degan cried out of his one good eye.

In the morning he noticed a terrible smell in the room. "I stink," he told the nurse. "I smell like I'm dead," he told Ravishani.

"We have altered the events so that you may have a liquid cleansing this forenoon."

Three nurses dragged him out of bed and into a wheelchair. They washed him with a sponge.

"I don't stink anymore," he told Lill and Teddy that afternoon.

"Good, Grandpa." Degan saw Lill flash Teddy a menacing look. "Not that you stunk before, but you must be feeling...clean."

"They dress up corpses too. What are you going to wear when you die, Teddy? Jailhouse stripes? Lill, I bet you'll wear your bowling shirt. Mr. Karnikowski – under me, you know – he got buried in his gas-meter reader's uniform. His wife wanted it that way. Maybe I can be buried in my sentimental favorite, my bathrobe. And you know how they stuff your cheeks so you look robust? Remember how robust Fanny looked even though she weighed seventy-two pounds? Well, I was thinking they could stuff my pecker so that it sticks out of the coffin. Maybe it could be waving the flag of Israel."

"I'm going to get coffee," Lill said.

Degan winked at Teddy. "You know what, Teddy? Last night I tried to kill myself, but I couldn't because hospitals don't leave things around for you." Teddy cocked his head, listening. "They make you not die until you die. Then they say it's best you're dead because you suffered so. Makes sense, huh? So I was thinking, Ted, that I want you to do me a favor."

"Sure, Grandpa."

"I want you to bring something. Enough to kill me. If I get worse, that is."

"Grandpa, I can't. You'd die. I'd get arrested. It'd kill Mom."

"No one would know. Ravishani won't want an autopsy. Don't Indians believe we need our bodies to come back as flies?"

"I think so, but Grandpa..."

"Man to man, Ted. Please."

Degan thought he felt something on his left side. His heart pounded. Then he realized that it was his right side that was on fire. His toes burned and were gone. The fire consumed his leg and rose to his chest and arm. "I'm dying," he said, but no one was in the room.

When Degan regained consciousness, Dr. Ravishani was standing over him. "I am sorry, Mr. Degan, that you are again the victim. The blood lacks consideration. You are stationary, moreover."

"I want Teddy," Degan whispered, this time with huge effort. Teddy's name came out as "I ask."

Lill and Teddy came into the room. Degan could see that Lill had been crying. "Yawn," he said to Teddy, meaning *now*. "I'm slurp," Degan said and closed his eyes.

He heard a noise in the room. Then David Letterman said good night. It must be midnight. Teddy's face floated above his. He could see the longish jaw that was also his, but Teddy's face lacked the meanness that gave his focus.

"I brought some stuff," Teddy whispered close to his ear, "and a needle. It won't take long, but you have to promise that this is what you want. You have to say it, Grandpa. And mean it."

"Yes, please, Teddy. I can't see the sense. It's time," was what he wanted to say. Teddy heard "peas" and "factory" and "yes."

"I'm giving you morphine, Grandpa. A friend gave it to me. It's pure and won't hurt." Teddy squeezed above his grandfather's elbow, and a vein popped out. The needle went in easily in a recent needle mark, and Degan felt all the warmth and pleasure he had ever known, swimming yellow pleasure, like peeing in bed. "Thank you" came out "can't."

DON'T SEND POEMS,
SEND MONEY

I AM TALKING TO my friend Lori. We go back to high school, though our relations have sometimes been strained by small acts. When she changed the spelling of her name at fifteen to the then fashionable *i* ending, when I decided not to be a scientist, when my child Sari was born (Oh, how time changes one's attitude toward spelling!), there was a wedge between us. "Do you think we'll ever get along?" I once asked her. "Why should we?" she replied, and I am sure she wasn't teasing. Lori hadn't understood the problem suggested by the question. That's the way she is.

Today Lori is on speed that an old doctor friend "lent" her. He lends her drugs. Sometimes on Sundays Lori lends his girlfriend her roller skates. It's all very congenial, considering that Lori and the doctor were lovers for seven years. At the end of their affair, he said, "Sorry, I found someone I really like."

Lori is upset. She bites her lower lip and sucks in her cheeks and stirs her coffee so that it slaps against the rim. She still isn't married, which isn't a problem, I assure her. I am married. Am I always happy? Has marriage changed me? Lori is sure that the man intended for her died somewhere in Little League. "He probably played second base, and one day a stinging liner got him in the Adam's apple." That's something else about Lori. She likes using baseball as a metaphor for life. When she had an abortion, it was "like sliding home without kneepads." When my father died, she kept repeating, "How can a Cubs fan die?" I'm not kidding.

65

Well, what should she do, she's asking, be a widow all her life?

"How can you be a widow when you've never been married?"

She ignores me. "Go out and face the sea? Always wear black? Light a candle every year? Never sleep with another man? Act damn decorous?"

She's biting her lip furiously. I want her to stop. "Did I ever tell you about my mother?" I ask. My mother is a real widow, but that's beside the point. "Whenever she gets the notice from the funeral home that my father's *Yahrzeit* is coming up, she goes out and buys a commemorative candle the same day. The notice is sent a month ahead, but the day it arrives, she burns the candle. She doesn't want to connect the candle with his death. She just wants to get the thing over with."

Lori is looking past me. She avoids me with her pale green eyes, the color of the candy-coated almonds one eats only at movies. "So?" she says and smarts. "You're married. Your mom was married. My mother is married. I'm thirty-four. Your daughter is growing breasts, and I'm not married."

"Sari is precocious," I try to console her.

That strikes her. I'm reminded of those old horror movies in which the mere act of brushing one's shoulder against a wall sets it spinning, revealing a secret room filled with horrible skulls.

Lori explodes. "Is that supposed to be funny?" We're sitting at the Désirée Coffee Shop, and suddenly Anne the waitress and Spirow the cashier are wondering too. "Is it funny to you, Elaine, that my life is half over, that I'll never have children, and that someone who's been married two hundred years is telling me that marriage isn't important?"

I should be quiet and reverent at a time like this. I should eat my doughnut or look at the clock's cartoon hands or tap out *"Que Será Será"* on the silver laminated counter, but I don't understand keeping a low profile. I've always been

66

able to cheer Lori, until today, and I can't stop trying now.

"Twelve years, Lori, and it's just a training bra."

"What are they in training for?" Lori scowls at her age-old joke. She's trying to be brave.

"Look, Lori," I begin. "I know you'd like to get married, but don't be like my mother. Wait until the act has meaning for you. Hell, if you just want to marry anyone, it can be accomplished in three months. It's quality you want."

"I'm not so sure," Lori says and stares at the geometric display of Winstons behind the counter. We're both getting older. Lori's mouth has begun to turn down, and her cheeks seem puffy. My own hair is streaked with gray. Though Sari says it makes her worry I'll die soon, I like it, and Peter likes it. Besides, I connect dyed hair with Richard Nixon sweating through his TV pancake make-up. I picture myself at a concert — Berlioz, open air, late July. A leaf falls from a tree. I go to brush it off and come up with a handful of hair color. It's one of those nagging worries, like sitting on a bench marked WET PAINT, remote but statistically possible. I trace the fear back to the time I saw a homely, well-dressed woman chasing her French-rolled wig down State Street. Her own hair was thin and apricot-colored. It was pinned to her head with scores of black bobby pins, her skull resembling the aftermath of a forest fire. Graceful aging will be my forte, I decided long ago.

I hug Lori and go home, walking down side streets for seventeen blocks instead of taking the el. Spring is just starting to disfigure the trees, and the air smells ionized. On one corner three boys are chasing each other around and around in an ever smaller circle. If I watch them long enough, they might become one boy, occupying the same space at the same time, though Sari's natural-science book assures us it's an impossibility. That's one consolation of having children: you learn new things, or you learn the things you've forgotten. One summer I worked as a waitress. An older colleague told me about her mother in a nursing home. She had forgotten she had a daughter, so every time Donna visited, she had to reintroduce herself. And her mother always seemed pleased to meet her.

That night I tell Peter how depressed Lori seems. "Does she still see the roller-skating doctor?" he asks.

"Only to get pills now and then."

"Too bad," he mutters from the direction of the shower. He takes a shower before dinner. "Maybe she should advertise," he says.

"Are you serious?" I shout through three off-white rooms.

"Why not?" he asks. Then I hear water hissing, a stock-market report on the radio, and Sari knocking on the front door: three, the magic number.

At dinner Peter says, "She can say SWFRNRS desires A for marriage."

"What are all those initials, Dad?"

"Single white female registered nurse roller skater," Peter smiles.

Sari explodes in histrionic laughter. She rolls her eyes toward the ceiling. She covers her mouth. She ignores dinner.

"What's A?" I venture.

"Anyone," Peter says.

"Isn't it numb?" Sari asks.

"What?" I say.

"To be as old as Lori and not be married."

"Not really, if you can't find the right person, or if you're happier single." It bothers me that I'm raising a child with pronounced monogamous tendencies. I remember once that Sari told me she wanted to have five children, three boys and two girls and the girls last. I flew into a rage. I shouted out permutations on the figure that included twins, quintuplets, all boys, no boys, four girls, one boy. I ranted while Sari looked cool, waiting for me to subside. I hate that she's decided matters that are better left to chance.

Later the phone rings. It's Lori at the hospital, where she's a preemie intensive-care nurse. "It's slow tonight," she says. "All the babies either died or went home." I wonder if she says things like that when she meets men. I can see her sitting around the whirlpool at her expensive health club with its all-night salad bar featuring truffles. She pays two hundred dollars a month to belong. "What do you do?" asks a red-bearded guy with a racquetball bruise on his left forearm. "I wire small babies for sound." Oh, the odd looks, the hasty retreats!

"Lori," I ask, "how would you like to come to dinner Saturday? There's a new lawyer at Peter's office, just in from the coast. He wants to meet people, and Peter says he's very bright." I hold my breath, half-hoping she'll refuse, because Peter hardly knows the fellow, thinks he's superficial, and had an argument with him at the water cooler about a certain olive-green plastic tumbler.

"Fine," Lori says. "I'm off Saturday. Formal?"

"No, roller skates. I'll probably wear a dress."

"Red or white?"

"I hate red. It makes me look like a cow, and white is out before Memorial Day."

"I mean wine."

I hadn't thought. "Why not white?" I ask without considering, and instantly I'm committed to fish or fowl. The whole world of red meat is out of the question: no beef, pork, lamb, giraffe, or buffalo. Life is simpler now. That's how I like doing things, on impulse. Sari was one. So was Peter.

Maybe Lori's problem is that she considers too much. I can see her training her eye to watch the life signs of the preemies, this one cyanotic, that one born without a gullet. "If they live, it's hard. If they die, it's worse." The many nuances she has to be aware of. This one's respiration is one beat slower. That one spit up a microgram of blood. I'm glad I never became a nurse. I owe my marriage to it.

69

"Peter," I say, "since Christmas is over, it'll be seen as sheer kindness."

"What will?"

"Asking over the Larson fellow. I want him to meet Lori."

"He's a creep," Peter states, wiping his hair dry after running. Sweat is racing down his face. He looks as if he's crying. "Why do you want Lori to meet a creep?"

"Maybe your friends think I'm a creep."

"Probably," Peter whispers theatrically.

"Maybe she'll love him."

"When?"

"Next Saturday. It's her day off. She's bringing white wine."

"Good. I'll tell him to bring the main dish and dessert, and we'll go out."

"Funny," I say. "I can make that bouillabaisse."

"No," Peter says. "Larson has a beard."

"So?"

"Bouillabaisse is too messy to eat. I don't want Lori to indict him on table manners."

"Well, I can make a crab-meat quiche and cook it very well. I can make a salad and chop the spinach leaves very small. I can make a chocolate mousse but leave off the whipped cream. Then Larson can have no embarrassments."

"Mike."

"Larson, Mike. Is he really a creep?"

"Nothing he's done at work indicates otherwise."

"I hope I'm doing the right thing," I say and go make Sari's lunch for school. Sari is in a rut. Every day she orders the same things: cream cheese and sprouts on whole wheat, a tangelo, and a granola bar. If we were in a fallout shelter, that's all Sari would accept for lunch. I hear Peter making a call in the other room. He sounds jovial. Larson, Mike, must be accepting.

I can remember the first time Lori met Peter. He and I had

70

practically been living together for a month. I kept all my clothes in two neat shopping bags in a corner of his bedroom. He was beginning law school. I had all my credits in science but wasn't interested. "But my dad is a chemist," I'd whisper in bed. "You don't have to be your dad," he'd tell me. Peter has serious eyes. I believed him.

Lori met us after dinner that night. Nixon had just invaded Cambodia. We went to a sit-in and then spent the night together being processed in an ultramodern urban jail with track lighting, where the policemen looked younger than we did and just as nervous.

"Larson says okay. I told him seven o'clock. He didn't ask what color wine."

"Inconsiderate," I say and stuff Sari's "Annie" lunch box into the refrigerator. A piece of wilted lettuce rests on Sandy the dog's ear.

The week goes quickly. I'm working on a story for a woman's magazine about battered husbands. Today I'm scheduled to interview yet another, a man whose wife once broke his arm.

I wonder why I always feel nervous before these meetings. After all, I didn't do anything to any of these poor fellows. I've never so much as pinched Peter under the dinner table for revealing that I was pregnant with Sari when we got married. I'm to meet the man at a local restaurant specializing in ribs. Thinking of the difficulty of interviewing and eating ribs at the same time, I've already decided on a salad. He told me that he has brown hair and a lighter mustache. I realize, as I'm surveying the room, that I'm looking for someone wounded. For some reason I always picture a Revolutionary War Minuteman with a fife and a bloodied headband. I've told him I'll be wearing a gray trench coat, though the day is unseasonably warm and I'm sweating. Anxiously I wait, doing my duty. A tall man approaches.

"Hello. You must be Elaine."

"Nice meeting you," I say and extend my hand, pressing his ever so gently.

We sit down and order. The waitress acts very polite and consoling, as if she knows this is no ordinary lunch. My salad arrives, his ribs, my lite beer, his bourbon on the rocks, and we begin. It all happened eight years ago when he was a law student.

"My husband was a law student too," I tell him.

"Oh yeah? Where?"

"Chicago. Class of seventy-four."

"Me too," he says.

"That *is* strange," I say. "When did your wife begin her actions?" I smile nervously. I sound too indirect, tentative. It's more like a class reunion.

"What's your husband's name?" he asks.

"Peter Rediger."

"I know him," Mr. X says. I never ask their names, to assure confidentiality. "We used to go out for a beer now and then. He was seeing this weird woman. She had a degree in physics, but she didn't want to do anything with it. So she got pregnant."

"Really?" I say and call for another beer.

"So they got married and he was in law school and she was having a career crisis, and meanwhile Peter had to support a family and go to school. Then she decided that she wanted to be an artist, knit rugs or something. So she got a little part-time job for pin money, but it was all on Peter. I'm surprised he was able to do so well in school."

I realize three things. First, I'm writing down everything he's saying about me. Second, I'm some shade of burnt mauve. And third, I might abuse him, given the chance.

"So you're Peter's second wife."

I brace myself and dig in. "No, I'm the first."

"Oh," he says and coughs quietly. "I have this memory that won't quit."

"Your best quality, I'm sure." I try to begin again. "How

72

was it that your wife began to *abuse* you?" I even stress the word.

"We had no money. She wanted things. I couldn't give them to her."

"What was she doing at the time?"

"She was in school too. Getting an M.F.A. in art history. She was studying Giacometti."

"I always loved Giacometti."

"Shadows," he says bitterly. "Little spidery shadows. I'd want dinner when I came home. She never had it ready because she was reading some new work on Giacometti. We'd fight. Once I threatened to take her books and burn them, and she went wild. She pulled my hair and slapped me and kicked me on my knee."

"Did you try to defend yourself?" I ask. He is a tall, well-proportioned man.

"Sure I did, but not really. I didn't want to go and deck my wife. So she's kicking and screaming *she* never liked me, her parents liked me, and I pick up her book and throw it out the window."

"The window?"

"We lived on the fourteenth floor of student housing. Then she goes insane. Our little studio becomes a carnival booth. She's throwing dishes and tearing at place mats and spilling talcum all over the place, and I can't stop her. So I slapped her."

"You slapped her?"

"Yeah. She was like the Hulk. She's overturning chairs. She's small, maybe a hundred pounds, but she's doing something funny to the hide-a-bed, and it's not even ours. I thought slapping her would help. All of a sudden she takes my arm and twists it behind my back, and I'm on the carpet seeing the Milky Way. Then she gets all concerned and takes me to Billings Hospital, and they set it."

"Did they ask you how it happened?"

"Yeah, but I just said it was an accident."

73

"Then what happened?"

"I went home, took a pain pill, went to sleep, and in the morning she was gone. She'd moved back in with her parents."

"Did you reconcile?"

"No. That was it." Now he chews furiously on a rib and seems finished.

"Would you say the pressure of being in college and being married got to both of you?"

"We all do things differently. Some people throw books out windows. Others get pregnant and don't become physicists."

"Chemists. And it was writing."

"Yeah. We all do it differently."

I start thinking of Lori. No wonder she's so selective. I politely thank him, offer to pay for his lunch, leave eight dollars to cover my share when he refuses, and go home. It's already four o'clock, and I should go shopping for groceries, but I feel wiped out. Chances are I'd forget half the items. So I go home and lie on my bed. Sari is in her room playing her "Annie" record. "The sun'll come up to-mo-ro-o-ow" repeats itself over and over. Apparently she's fallen asleep before taking it off her kids record player.

A while later I hear water running and know that Peter's home. He bends down and kisses me. I notice that he still wears his wedding ring, and suddenly I feel better. I really can't blame him for Mr. X. Nevertheless, I feel curious.

Peter is peeling off a tie raining umbrellas, a pink button-down, a sweaty T-shirt, then gray flannel slacks, beige socks. He's down to his shorts when I say, "I ran into an old friend of yours."

"Really?" he asks. "Where?"

"He was one of my abused husbands."

"Hard to believe. What's his name?"

"You know I don't know their names," I say too sharply, "though he seemed to know a lot about me. He said he used

74

to drink with you and he admired you for doing so well in school despite your unfortunate marriage to a woman who was going to be a physicist but turned out a mother."

Peter sits next to me on the bed. He looks embarrassed. "The creep said that?"

"Yep."

"It's all surmise and misinterpretation, Elaine."

"I believe you, Peter," I say. "Besides, it's too long ago to matter. You can't be responsible for every jerk you've known."

Peter seems relieved. He kisses me lavishly and does a little naked pirouette on the way to the shower.

I wake up and go into Sari's room. She's fallen asleep in my old negligée and Grandma's satin slippers. She's wearing rouge, lipstick, and a fan barrette from the fifties. Her little record player wobbles on and on at the foot of her bed. I turn it off, and she continues to sleep.

The next morning I go shopping for our dinner party that night. Despite Lori's promised white wine, there's a sale on rolled rib roasts, so I buy one and Idaho potatoes to bake and chives for the sour cream and fresh wax beans and ingredients for a lemon meringue pie. My interview with Mr. X has made me nostalgic for what I used to cook, my Sunday best, a roast.

When I get home, Sari is manipulating her Rubik's cube without even looking. She is watching one of those reassuring kids-are-likewise-human Saturday morning shows. They're interviewing the youthful editor of a magazine that prints writing "of children, by children, and for children." "And how should kids in our TV audience send to your magazine?" the cheeky emcee asks. "Don't send poems, send money," the twelve-year-old with the Frankenstein forehead and shiny glasses says. "We need to establish a broader base." Do children have to be shaken down so young, I wonder.

Peter is reading some office work. They're involved in a

big case against a paper manufacturer that's polluting Lake Michigan, the kind of case that he rarely wins but that makes him feel good about himself for weeks. I kiss him and say, "Tonight it's Sunday Dinner Revisited, Old Cuisine, Return to University Place."

"Huh?" he says. When Peter's concentrating on a case, he hears one-eighth of what I'm saying. Of those words he might have caught "Sunday."

"I'm making a roast."

"Fine," he says and looks back at the documents.

At seven o'clock Mike Larson is scheduled to arrive. I've hardly thought about him or Lori all week, which is the problem with dinner parties. By the time they take place, their original impulse is lost. It's like sending a Christmas card into space and hoping an alien finds it on the right date. That's why they send chemical equations and geometric shapes.

At six-thirty Peter is scheduled to take Sari to Julia's for the night. There they'll make popcorn, read each other's diaries, and whisper about Julia's mom's new live-in boyfriend. Sari told me he imports something, but she didn't remember the word. "It must be foreign," she said. Then one night she said, "Lookahs."

"Hookahs?" I asked. Julia's mom has a Ph.D. in histology, and she's dating a pusher. Oh well. Sari assures me they're very polite to her and make the girls go to bed by ten.

Before Peter gets back, the doorbell rings. If I'm lucky, it'll be Lori a little early. I'm not lucky. A tall bearded man is standing at our front door. The porch light is broken, and in the dimness all I'm able to see is his beard, only I imagine it covered with food, decorated as a Christmas tree.

"Won't you come in?" I ask.

"Thanks. I'm Mike."

"Larson," I add to show expertise.

"And you must be..."

"Elaine. Elaine Rediger." It's a reflex to say both, though I know he knows my last name.

"Come in and have a drink. What would you like?"

"Vodka on the rocks. Where's Peter?"

"Driving our daughter to a friend's. He'll be back any minute."

The doorbell rings again. Certainly it's Peter. I ask Mike to get the door while I make the drinks. I'm in the kitchen for a long time before I hear voices, one male and one female. It is Lori. She looks as if she's been routed from her apartment by fire before she could finish dressing. Her hair is wet. She's wearing a pretty maroon dress that looks like silk but with penny loafers and no make-up.

"I thought I'd be late," she says apologetically. "May I use your washroom?"

"Be my guest," I say. "Oh, Lori, have you...?"

"Yes, we met."

Larson and I sit down to share a drink. He tells me Peter is a fine lawyer and an enthusiastic worker. I feel as if I'm meeting his civics teacher or the commandant of his prison camp. I'm stirring some vermouth and waiting for Larson to speak, when he chokes. His face turns scarlet, his cheeks puff out, his eyes water. He looks like a fearsome fish from Sari's animal encyclopedia. "Are you all right?" I ask, knowing he can't answer. Then the phone rings.

I go to the phone, half-thinking Larson's going to die on us, but even as I leave the room, it gets quiet, and I hear him draw a deep breath. I pick up the phone.

"It's me," Peter says. He sounds as if he has a mask on.

"Where are you?" I ask.

"At the hospital."

"Why?" I ask. I can feel my heart accelerate.

"After I dropped off Sari, a guy rear-ended me at a stoplight. I'm really okay, but I hit my lip and the cut seemed deep, so I went to the hospital and they're going to sew it up."

My stomach turns. I see an ocean of Peter's blood.

"Do you want me to come over?" I ask, thin-voiced.

"I'm really okay, Elaine. It just needs four or five stitches and I'll be home. It's a busman's holiday for me."

"What do you mean?"

"I get to chase my own ambulance."

"Did they take you in an ambulance?" I ask, heart dare-deviling.

"Just a joke, honey. Have a drink. I'm fine. I'll be home as soon as I can."

When I get to the front room, Lori has poured herself some tonic and looks finished. She has switched to gray sandals, and her hair is perfectly dry.

"That was Peter," I say. "He had a little accident, but he's okay. His lip needs a few stitches. It's nothing to be alarmed about." Neither guest seems alarmed, so I decide to minimize it. "Speaking of stitches," I say, "Lori is a nurse."

Lori shrugs and nods the way Sari does when I announce that she can play Chopin.

"I think Peter told me," Larson says. He has stopped choking and has returned to his normal hue, a faintly tanned, rosy one.

"Do you jog?" Lori asks him.

"I never took it up," Larson says. And then a few seconds later he remembers he should ask her. "Do you?"

"I used to, but then I joined the Mid-Center Health Club, and I've taken up swimming. I swim seventy laps four days a week."

Larson says nothing, concentrating on his drink. I wonder if he's recovered from his accident.

"Lori and I met in high school," I say. "She was always a good athlete."

She nods politely. "And Elaine was always a brain. She was going to be an astronomer."

"Chemist," I correct.

Larson smiles. "I once wanted to be a pilot."

"Me too," says Lori, "only I wanted to be a stewardess."

I look at the two, Ken and Barbie, only Barbie is a little jowly and Ken is subject to fits of choking. I excuse myself and go into the kitchen to work on the dinner. Lori's forgotten the wine she promised, so there'll be no problems with the red-meat issue.

"I hope you both like roast," I shout from the kitchen, thinking how odd it is to hope such a thing. I'm reminded of those signs that say EAT HERE or give other obvious advice. This is America, 1982, and though we may not eat as much, we all like roast.

Larson walks into the kitchen. He is very thin and has deep brown eyes. "There's a problem," he says. "I'm sorry that Peter didn't mention to you" — and here I imagine him confessing that he's an ex-abused husband — "that I'm somewhat of a vegetarian." I look him over, try to check his belt to see if it's made of animal hide, look for signs of falseness about his hair. If he's a Hare Krishna, I'll throw him out on his ear. A few years ago they were everywhere, at airports, tollbooths, the gynecologist, but I can't imagine that one would turn up in my house. "I eat fish," Larson says, "but not roast."

"That's okay," I say. "I have some tofu in the refrigerator or cream cheese with sprouts."

"Please don't make any extra effort," he says, hand resting on some of Sari's refrigerator art.

"Are you sure?" I ask, picturing his nearly empty plate.

"Sure," he says. "May I have another drink?" I hear a car door slam and a key tumbling in the lock. Peter is home, mended. He walks in. I hear him saying a muffled hello to our guests. Then he enters the kitchen. His upper lip is swollen to twice its size and stitched together with what resembles shoelace.

"Can you eat?" I ask him.

"I don't think so," he slurs. "It's full of Novocaine."

"Are you hungry?" I ask Lori.

79

"Not really," she says, eyes focused on Peter's prominent lip. "A good job," she says.

"Lori used to be a surgical nurse," I add. Lori gives me a smiting glance. I'm supposed to stop doing her press releases. "Well, since I'm the only one who's eating, why don't we do something else? The food will keep. It's no problem."

"How about a movie?" Lori asks.

"Fine with me," Larson says.

"Okay," Peter says, "as long as someone else drives."

We walk out to Larson's car. Lori and Larson get into the front seat, Lori sitting as close to her door as she can. Peter and I sit in back, close to each other and silent. I watch Lori watching Larson. He's telling her about the funny man who sold him the car. "He looked like his ears were on backward." Lori tilts her head back, thinking maybe she should smile. I sit next to Peter, his hand in mine. We don't know what movie to see. I feel as if I'm on a date with the guy who scored the winning touchdown for our team, only where is his letter sweater, my Angora-covered class ring? I plant a kiss on Peter's stitches, and he winces.

As Larson pulls away from the curb, Lori begins, "Did I ever tell you about the time Elaine and I were robbed at gunpoint?" Larson laughs too loud. It really isn't funny at all. "Of course I didn't," Lori answers. She looks glum. "I haven't told you anything."

HEROES

THE SUN, HAVING nothing to do, leaned in the window. Having still less to do, Harvey Brilligbusch watched it with perverse concentration. As usual, he was translating his name into English. Brightbush, he thought, lengthening the syllables, accenting the first, then the second, rhyming it with other words that came to mind: *light push*, *nightstick*, *tight lush*. He liked that better: Harvey Tightlush. And the fact that Rachel's last name translated to Black Sky should have been an omen.

The sun snapped into place on the crossword puzzle's forty-seven down, which was *salamander*. Why did the *Times* always use the same tired words? Harvey wrote *eft* in pen in the three spaces. He was never wrong about words. Downstairs, Belinda, a sturdy child with stout legs and crooked teeth, whom the divorce lawyer had given him for eight more summers, was twirling on the sidewalk. He hoped she wouldn't fall and bump her face or lacerate her lip or scrape her nose or chip her tooth or dislocate her jaw or die. The list of perils was endless if events went predictably. Rachel's daily calls, made in the high-pitched clip of a commentator at the Hindenburg disaster, were justified considering Belinda's post-divorce pattern. First it was a broken arm and then a stitched forehead. Rachel must have given her subliminal accident plans when she sent Belinda packing for the summer: Sustain injuries. Old Frightwish deserves it. Now Belinda ran down the sidewalk toward Caroline's house. The trouble with summers was that Harvey felt he spent most of his time leaning, waiting for something bad to happen, afraid to take his eyes off the window.

Now he felt hungry. That was his other summer problem. Since his divorce, summers provoked in him a terrible hunger, a monstrous hunger, a hunger beyond human possibility. He thought of the vegetable slime that carpeted the gorilla cage at Lincoln Park Zoo. His hunger was larger. And his wish for sex. During the academic year, he comported himself properly. Summers he wanted to prowl. He wanted to go to the beach, which he usually hated, which burned his forehead and back and legs. There he wanted to mount every woman under forty. No. That was unfair. He wanted to mount grandmothers, invalids being wheeled by their nurses, children too small to consider without a lurid shiver. Even men appealed to him in summer. Brightwish. It was love that he felt. He wanted to consume the world.

He tried to remember how he had felt in the summers before he and Rachel divorced. Whenever he tried to remember, he was a victim of partial amnesia. He was sure he had had a life then, but memories of it were as hazy as the photos of Nassau that Merle Dusback showed him at the faculty party. Upstairs, Dr. Christman had been so noisily humping Sandy Olesker, a pretty graduate student, that someone turned on a tape of German drinking songs to cover the groans. He knew he had never done crossword puzzles before or hungered so or lusted so. He had never watched where the sun decided to lean or cared if Belinda twirled on the sidewalk. "Stop it!" he shouted down to Belinda and Caroline, as they balanced on a low stone fence surrounding the front yard of his three-flat.

"What?" Belinda called up without looking, in her new manner of cautious independence.

"Get off the goddamned fence!" Both girls giggled up at him from the sidewalk.

It was already hot, and Harvey felt the sweat dripping down his temples, slithering down his chest, and beading under his beard. Maybe he should shave his beard, but it was part of the Brightbush image. Summer had just started, and he had already sweated more than he remembered ever sweating when he was married. Even when he and Rachel used to make love in the summer, he didn't remember sweating like this.

Belinda had been under his care for only three days, and already his temper was short with her. His study was in the back of the apartment, a place he seemed to haunt only at night with Belinda safely in bed. He couldn't consider going there now with Belinda so close to ruin. Now she and Caroline were tossing a Frisbee that might land on the street or under a moving truck. Chasing after it, Belinda resembled a cleaning lady going after a cobweb. Her friend Caroline was lovely, small-boned with boyish hips. Harvey blinked her away, then watched the sun sidle to another location on the table. It landed on the ashtray. So he smoked now, a new peccadillo Rachel would certainly remark on when she next visited. Did everything Harvey did have to mean something? Was it charged with significance that Rachel's new haircut resembled shredded lettuce, that she was in therapy, that she worked as a flight controller though her training was in philosophy? She would survey his life like a reconnaissance pilot. "A new ashtray?" "So it's bourbon?" "Since when do you buy *TV Guide*?" If she could line up all his new possessions and shoot them, she'd annihilate his existence since Rachel. And if he showed her something wonderful, his new article, for instance, she'd smile her "Merely clever." But Rachel had never been effusive. Why should she change now, especially after her declarations of hatred for him?

Belinda and Caroline disappeared around the corner shouting something about "park" and "lunch" and "later." As soon as she was out of sight, he could relax. Could he be responsible for her off of the block, renting bodyguards or stationing police at every intersection that a plain ten-year-old might cross? He could go back to his study and open the letter that Reitle had sent from Berlin. But he was too sweaty and wrung out to follow Reitle's German, even if it was news he wanted to hear, that the "new" Kafka work had been verified. No, he'd go ring Holly Noble's bell and see if she was eating lunch or wanting company.

Before he walked down the fourteen green shagged steps to Holly's, he would freshen up. He went to the bathroom and sprayed deodorant under his T-shirt. Then he saw the full moons of sweat staining the shirt and took it off. He looked swollen in the mirror. His eyes were smaller because his face was larger, and even his beard couldn't hide the new fullness of his cheeks. He looked like a round loaf of bread. God, he *was* repulsive. Rachel was right. He looked away quickly and went into the bedroom, thinking about Holly's cool and streamlined arms. Once they'd made love after they'd both had too much Bolla, but he couldn't remember much about it, only that in his excitement he had delivered too fast. She had seemed amused about it. In fact, Holly seemed amused about everything. Harvey tried not to think about her amusement. Sometimes it frightened him because he associated it with a lack of intelligence. He pictured her laughing through cathedrals and art museums, in hospitals, and at great works of literature, which he guessed she never read. He heard her giggling through *Heart of Darkness* and *Œdipus Rex*. Stop thinking that way, Tight Ass, he told himself. She's good for you, Tight Ass. Now he buttoned a blue Oxford-cloth shirt and put on a newly laundered pair of jeans and a belt with a jaunty red stripe and his tennis shoes and sprayed himself liberally with Adam, "the cologne that tempted Eve before the apple."

He took a bottle of Chablis from his refrigerator and jumped the stairs two at a time. Maybe he should have appeared at her door wearing a suit. She'd have giggled and said he was all suited up. Once she told him to see a nutritionist because he'd said he felt Byronic.

He knocked on the door. Inside he could hear a type-

84

writer's keys being slammed. That meant she was transcribing and probably had on her earphones. He wondered how she could work in a room hung with the quilts she had designed, none of which matched each other. The walls had the look of a Byzantine bazaar or of a bad trip. He knocked again. He heard the typewriter stop, and the door opened. Holly was dressed in cut-offs and a white T-shirt. Her hair hadn't been combed, and her feet were bare and dirty.

"What's this?" she smiled good-naturedly, pointing at the wine.

"I thought you might come up for lunch. I brought down a sample." He didn't know what he'd give her if she accepted, but he couldn't risk being downstairs too long with Belinda away. Tomorrow he'd give Belinda a key and tell her to let herself in and out. Maybe he could start spending lots of time at Holly's. And what would stop him from sleeping there? After all, he'd be closer to Belinda vertically than they'd be horizontally in the same apartment.

"But I have so much to do, Harve."

She called him Harve, which reminded him of *starve*. That depressed him, but, after all, his name did mean *bitter*. Holly, on the other hand, didn't remind him of Christmas but of *collie*. She was thin and fine-boned and sad-eyed as pets in children's books. When she smiled, which she did often, her teeth were even pointed like a dog's. Her hair was the honey color of a golden retriever's, and the few times she had been in his apartment, she had followed him from room to room as dogs do. If he were a man prone to using endearments, he might have called her "pet." Once he had called Rachel "little bird," mainly because her features were sharp and drawn, and she had said, "Drop dead."

"Tell you what. I'll come up in an hour after I finish this report. I'll bring some fruit." She laughed. He wondered why fruit was funny. "I just bought some huge strawberries. Oh, and by the way, I'd love to meet your daughter." That was funny to her too.

"She's somewhere," he said.

"Okay. I'll be up at two. Now don't eat without me." Then her quick canine smile. Why would he eat without her? Could she sense his hunger? Then she waved three times and said "Bye!" twice and closed the door. He stood there listening to her type, not wishing to go back alone to his apartment. Maybe he'd open the wine and drink it on the stairs. No, he'd save the wine for her. Comportment. Discipline. Instead, he'd go up and have a beer or three and try to concentrate on Reitle's letter.

The apartment was sweltering. Harvey tried sitting at the kitchen table to catch the cross breeze between the two open windows. The curtains swayed as curtains are supposed to sway. He had bought curtains not because he liked them but because he hated how depressing divorced men's apartments look. He didn't want to be part of the generic description of ex-husbands. Reitle's letter looked very thin. He balanced it in his hand, weighing what it might contain. Some kids were shouting in the alley. They reminded him of Belinda, who had been gone a full half-hour. Suppose she had been killed by a stray bullet or impaled on the monkey bars by a worker's flying fence spike?

"Come on, faggot, throw the ball!" one boy shouted.

"Your mother's a dyke," the other answered.

"Fuck yourself blind."

A noble aspiration, Harvey thought.

The bell rang, probably Belinda home just in time to ruin lunch with Holly. Harvey buzzed her in, thinking of ways to get even with Rachel for the next eight summers. Maybe he could have sex manuals sent to her address or a continuous stream of unordered pizzas. The feet on the stairs were too heavy to be Belinda's, and the voice was Alf Lester's, which obviously rhymed with *pester*. Harvey missed his ex-colleague, who had been denied tenure on the basis of his "creative" dissertation, *The Leap-Second, Beckett, and Me*. Now he was a part-time instructor at a local Cambodian

Refugee Center and a novelist, though he'd never finished any of his novels. When Harvey had questioned Alf about what he taught to the Cambodians, Alf had answered, "What's the difference? They need to learn everything." Harvey pictured the preliterate Hmong tribesmen debating poststructuralism. "I'm glad you're home, Harvey. I have a great idea for a novel. It's very Márquezian."

"Want a beer?"

"No, I have to teach in an hour." Harvey was relieved that Alf would be gone when Holly arrived. Harvey was sweating again. His shirt was darkening. He could feel little rivulets under his beard. He thought of Holly and imagined he could hear her typewriter tapping downstairs.

"The idea is that an Eastern European explorer in the sixteenth century sets out to discover a new spice route. I'm calling him Balto. *The Adventures of Balto Prisbic.* Anyway, Balto ends up in South America, where he's turned on to hallucinogens by a tribe of Indians, and the rest of the novel deals with Balto's cultural hallucinations."

"The unreliable narrator."

"Right. He thinks their culture is highly complex and advanced over his own, but we can never be sure whether he's hallucinating the ceremonies that take place or not. It'll be a study in the ritual of the imagination. Of course, before he gets there, his boat will be beset by pirates, people will die of cholera. You see, only Balto will get off that ship alive. I can't risk other characters complicating the narrative."

"Aren't most of the Eastern European countries landlocked?"

"Well, he can sign on under a British or Spanish flag. Probably Spanish in homage to Cervantes."

"Of course."

"I can go into his adventures along the way. You know, the whole picaresque thing. Inns. Coaches. Villains. Knights. The part that really interests me, though, is what kind of hallucinations a sixteenth-century mind might have. They'd have to deal with God, of course, but maybe Balto could be ahead of his times. Maybe his voyage could be a discovery of ideas to, say, existentialism."

"It sounds promising, Alf, but the more you discuss ideas with me, the less you ever get written. I'm telling you that as a friend. You know what Rachel used to say about you?"

"No worse than what she said about you."

"That you're potential energy divided by chattiness."

"She said that?"

"Why do you sound so awestruck?"

"Maybe Balto can say that in the book."

"He'd better not. Rachel would sue."

Alf appeared more serious now, which made him sink into himself, his clothes growing larger and the lines coming out on his face. Over the years Alf, Harvey noticed, had gotten sparer, while Harvey had grown robust, making him feel guilty in front of his friend. "Tell me, Alf, did I use to sweat like this in the old days?"

"I can't remember, Harvey."

Harvey was feeling insanely hungry. "Want a nice bologna sandwich, Alf?" He liked feeding Alf, whose salary barely kept him in rice and beans.

"Sure."

Now Harvey wouldn't have to wait for Holly to eat. His hunger was a deep, twisting ache that cut him from navel to groin. If Alf hadn't been there, he would have eaten the meat right from the package and gulped down the bread afterward to save time. "Why does meat have to be inside bread for it to be a sandwich? Why aren't two pieces of bread on one plate and two pieces of meat on another called a sandwich?"

"A problem of conjunction," Alf smiled.

"Alf, what would you take to a deserted island?"

Alf smiled, acknowledging the historical allusion. It was a topic both of them had used as graduate students teaching composition to the supposedly bright group. The ones who'd wanted A's had answered "great books." The really clever ones said "drugs." The future lawyers all said, "I wouldn't consent to go to a deserted island" and stated their rights.

"I'd take my bed," Alf said. "I can't sleep anywhere else."

"Know what I'd take?" Harvey smiled. "You."

"What's that in your hair?" Harvey asked Holly. She laughed and glanced up from the sink where she was slicing strawberries, peaches, and grapes into a fruit salad. Holly had changed into a red and white flowered sun dress under which she wore no bra. Standing to the side, he could see her breasts through the silk-screen pattern. "No, I mean it. I don't understand what holds back your hair."

"I think it's so nice," she said, "that your daughter is able to stay for summers. It's so important not to lose touch." She smiled at him.

Could teeth be sexy? Could hair fasteners be sexy? Could fingers daubed in strawberry juice be sexy? "Listen, Holly. Let's go to the bedroom. It's cooler in there, and I'm kind of full. My friend Alf was over. He looked so hungry I offered him a sandwich."

"And you ate too. Harve, you shouldn't have."

It was a lie that he wasn't hungry anymore. He didn't want to frighten her by shoveling in all the fruit and then going on to the powdered sugar until it landscaped his beard.

"How old is she?"

"Who?" Harvey asked, walking backward down the hallway toward the bedroom.

"Your daughter."

"Ten, but she's at the park."

"You're very lucky."

"I know. We can be alone now."

He heard her talking from the kitchen in the serious voice a teacher uses to address an audience full of high-school seniors. "I didn't get to see my father at all after my parents divorced. My father moved to Reno. Did you ever visit Reno? It's one big desert with some restaurants stuck in it. My father owns a restaurant there. I always picture him in the same coffee shop, with pink and white counters and a beige cash register. Don't ask me why it's always those colors."

He hadn't intended to ask. He could hardly hear her for all her effort through the asthmatic humming of the air conditioner. "It's cool in here," he called.

Holly came toward him, balancing the fruit salad, two forks, powdered sugar, and the bottle of wine on a tray. "Look! A movable feast!"

"I'm really not hungry."

"Of course," Holly said, irritation in her voice for the first time. A thin line of sweat marched across her upper lip. She placed the tray on the floor.

"Is it always this hot in summer?"

"I think so."

"I don't remember it being this damn hot, except in New Orleans once. As soon as you got into the car, the windows would sweat."

"That's humidity," Holly offered.

"Right, humidity." She was still standing over him. He touched her lightly on the back.

"Did you travel much with your wife?"

"To Europe once, and we planned a trip to China."

"I'd love to visit China. I hear it's very interesting."

He took her hand and pulled her toward him on the bed. Smiling so that her face shifted sideways, she said, "No, Harve." He let her go.

"China is very interesting. But then again, so is Ohio."

"Do you think that if I went to Reno I could find him? You know, no heartfelt scene, just tell him who I am, have a cup of coffee, and chat."

"Sure you could. Remember, it's women who change their names, not men."

"Isn't that strange? I've always liked my name." She sucked on the insides of her cheeks and looked over him toward the door, as if someone were standing there. To the door phantom she said, "You know, Harvey, I'd like to see more of you, but it has to be different than this."

"This?"

"You know."

"Well, we could go to interesting places. Have you ever been to Montreal? They speak French there."

"I took French in college. You speak several languages, don't you?"

"French, German, Old English, Latin — but not too many Romans to address these days." Shut up, he told himself.

"I was an art major in college," she said. "Sculpture. I began with pottery but found wood a more expressive medium."

"Wood's really solid."

"You know, Harve, I should be working. I'm losing money by not working this afternoon."

Sweat was starting again. It slid down his back in long discrete trails. He turned off the light and closed his eyes. "I'm tired, Holly, and you're losing money, and besides, this afternoon isn't really very interesting."

As soon as she was gone, he knew. Everything was too thin: the air in the room, his patience, Reitle's unopened letter. It had to be bad news. A letter confirming the Kafka stories and proposing his American editorship would contain plans, provisions, multiple copies. He opened his eyes, thought of reading the letter but decided to wait. Closing them again, his body took him deeper into his misery.

The doorbell rang and Harvey jumped up, head drumming. He always awoke with alarm, as though without his attention the world had fallen into ruin, war breaking out on the next block. When Rachel taught nights in the early years of their marriage, he'd had a phobia about falling asleep before she came home. Suppose he woke up and she still wasn't there? It wasn't her loss that he feared suffering. It was the pain of being so horribly surprised. He collected himself. Where was Belinda? He guessed he'd been sleeping for nearly an hour because the room had grown chilly and he felt the mottled bumpy flesh on his arms. Leaning long on the buzzer, he wondered what her excuse would be. Maybe he could return her to Rachel a little early, saying some scholarly business in Germany required his immediate attention.

He heard two voices on the stairs, Belinda's saying, "Home, Daddy?" and another voice saying something to Belinda. A flight down he could see his daughter slogging up the stairs, muddy and wet, followed by a policeman. Had she been rolled in the park? Was she injured?

His breath whistled. "What's the matter?"

"Nothing to get alarmed about, Mr. ...?"

"Harvey Brilligbusch."

"That's a strange name. German?"

"Yes."

"I'm German too. Family changed its name, though. We used to be Bleistift."

"*Pencil*?"

"Officer Pencil. Imagine that! Now we're Schmidt."

"What happened?"

"I just thought you'd want to know that your daughter's a real hero."

Harvey looked at Belinda's tentative smile. "What did she do?"

"Do you want to tell him?"

"No, you," Belinda said. Her face was streaked with mud. Her braids were soaking wet.

"Your daughter and her friend are by the lagoon. You know, where kids sail their boats and dogs swim. I tell kids, 'Stay out of that water. It's not for swimming.' Lots of bacteria."

"Right."

"So your daughter and the other little girl are at the playground going on swings, monkeying around. There's even some teeter-totters in it. You don't see as many as you used to. They're a little dangerous. See, kids don't think. They just do. A little boy wanders off from his day-care group. A little black boy about three. What's his name?"

"Carlos."

"Well, maybe he's Puerto Rican then. Puerto Rican is different."

"Please. What happened?"

"Little Carlos wanders off. No criticism, mind you, of the park personnel. So he's walking toward the lagoon. Then he sees a dog in the lagoon. Now I'm just guessing at this part, but I bet he decides he wants to swim out to that dog. So he wades in. And the water isn't blue. It's brownish. And little Carlos is dark."

Harvey could see Belinda getting nervous. He watched her tapping a soggy shoe.

"These two girls see little Carlos, and then they don't see him anymore. They still see the dog he was swimming to. Of course, three-year-olds can't really swim. Now I hate to think of this part. What do you see? You see a little boy sinking in the dirty water. He's going to drown. But your girl jumps in wearing her pretty pink shorts."

"Lilac," Belinda murmurs.

"She swims out toward the dog. She surface-dives in and out. It's not too deep, so she's able to find him and carry him out of the water. Meanwhile, her friend runs and gets me. I'm in the field house eating my lunch. And when we get back, she's giving him mouth-to-mouth resuscitation. How did you learn that?"

"On TV."

"So I get there and take over. The kid's coughing up water and crying. His teacher is crying. Lots of people are standing around. And can you beat this? Someone has called a mini-cam."

"I got interviewed, Daddy."

"So she's a hero. It'll be on the news tonight. You can tell the wife you really have one special kid."

Harvey followed Belinda into the apartment, where she went silently into the bathroom and locked the door.

"Clean up!" he shouted to her. He knew she was already doing that, but he had the habit of ordering people to do what they were already doing. "And then come out. I want to talk to you."

He walked into the kitchen and opened the letter. As he'd expected, it said that the Kafka stories couldn't be verified. Of course, that didn't mean they weren't Kafka stories, but one couldn't base an entire book on an argument from ignorance. Reitle was "profusely sorry" that they couldn't collaborate on a project whose results would have been "a harvest from the magical orchard." There was still the possibility of doing a study of veracity, the "truth of posthumous works." There'd be Dickinson's poems, "the fertile fields of Joyce," and, of course, a chapter on the alleged Kafka stories. Harvey was to respond in September, when Reitle returned from Rhodes. Meanwhile, he wished "dear Dr. Brilligbusch a sunny summer of endeavor."

Belinda walked into the kitchen wearing a bathrobe. Her face had the shiny wet look of a rubber bath toy.

"Daddy, should we call Mom and tell her? Won't she be proud?"

Sweating again, watching the stupid curtains, he looked at his child and thought she might disappear.

"She'll say I wasn't watching you. She'll have you all year. Why did you have to save him?"

94

THE HILLS
OF ANDORRA

WHEN MR. EWELL hired us, he spoke of three prohibi-
tions: late arrivals, early departures, and consorting with
the clientele. "Consorting" was the word he used, evoking
black garters and women spies obscured by fog. Every
waitress at the Silver Rooster was suspect. Mariel and I,
younger by ten years, college-educated, part of the dwindling
counterculture of the midseventies, were below suspicion.
What would women who wore no make-up, who didn't
shave their legs, who probably thought a Tía Maria was a
grenade used by Che in the Bolivian jungle, want with
paunchy businessmen doused in English Leather? I was
twenty-three, finishing my thesis on Beckett. Mariel was
twenty-four, trying to finance her journey westward to California, where James, the man she lived with, might pursue
his set-designing career. His career was all Mariel's idea. At
home James was happy painting detached human forms on
their bedroom walls while Mariel supported him. I wanted
to tell Mr. Ewell that it was James, not Mariel or I, who
needed a rich liaison: his tastes ran toward designer bath
sheets, Austrian goose comforters, and brioche for breakfast, served on a rattan tray.

Mariel and I had actually met earlier, in a college German
literature class, where the words slipped off her tongue, all
honey and smoothness. Though I was expert at understand-
ing, whenever I spoke the language, I felt insulted upon its
behalf, as if calling upon me was an error of inclusion.
Professor Hambling, raising his pointy chin and narrowing
his eyes, would concentrate on an invisible umlaut on the

ceiling. If my accent did anything, it betrayed my knowledge of Yiddish, learned from my grandmother. Mariel had been born in Germany after the war, of a displaced Lithuanian father and a mother who'd fled Dresden during the bombings. The family clung to each other as many refugees do, seeing their daily existence somehow in peril despite an ample bank account and roasts on the table. Everyone worked to send money back to relatives who had stayed in Frankfurt, whom Mariel would visit, bringing home lovely souvenirs to decorate her apartment: dishtowels embroidered with aphorisms about *Gemütlichkeit*, miniature finches tweeting atop a teapot when the water boiled, doilies scented in rose water, porcelain baby dolls, their curly hair the texture of corn silk.

Even at work Mariel was discriminating. While I fretted behind the waitress station for eating a forbidden muffin, Mariel pilfered whole steaks, etched sherry glasses, wicker wine stands. Maybe in the gray barracks of the D.P. camp where she had been born, her first feeling of deprivation had been an æsthetic one. Whatever the reason for her needs, she tried brazenly to satisfy them, sneaking past hotel security every night. Did her quilted purse contain special compartments for contraband? Happy as a prince, she'd display her daily plunder to me at the bus stop. Alone in my apartment after work, amid my useful possessions, paperback books, an oak writing desk, an aluminum teapot, I admired Mariel's style.

There is a theory that all public servants are frustrated performers. Why else did Anton, our maître d', add capers to the steak tartare so slowly that tension built? Why did Yvonne, a career waitress whose coif resembled a ruined birthday cake, fix her nylons in a mirror that customers might observe? And why did I practice applying Brandied Raisin lipstick, which I'd never worn before, in the bread knife's blade, as Yvonne had demonstrated that rainy, slow morning when Mariel didn't arrive until noon?

Yes, Mariel was often late, defying rule number one. And

sometimes she left early because of terrible menstrual cramps. She blamed them on her Catholic upbringing, the fears and cautions against showing one's legs, wearing silk underwear, and coming of age, as if someone could will otherwise. Having matured young, she felt the twisting ever after. Monthly she was doubled by it, bent sideways. Despite Anton's patience and my efficiency at covering two waitress stations, despite the painkillers Yvonne dispensed from her locker-room apothecary, Mariel would leave work early and creep to a cab to frighten the driver with her paleness, convinced that her womanhood was cursed.

Perhaps she was right. Three weeks after she was hired, Mariel was fired for breaking rule number three. Over coffee and stale sweet rolls in the employees' cafeteria, a veteran bellhop approached us. He needed a woman that night to act as "secretary" to a visiting manufacturer, to accompany him and a client to dinner and to make herself available afterward. The pay was two hundred dollars, all that Mariel needed to make her escape to California. "After you," we both teased each other, but as we joked, a feeling rose up in my stomach more sour than the warmed-over coffee. Mariel was considering the offer. I could tell by the way we stopped looking at each other.

Mariel never got to the floor that day. Apparently a house detective, one of those comical dog-eared, fray-cuffed, droopy-eyed snoops, caught wind of the deal before it was concluded. Later I imagined old Ewell lying in bed, his arthritic knees flaming, devising the plan to test his new employees. Mariel was hustled out of the hotel, warned never to return under penalty of law. The bellhop-turned-pimp got off free. At least they could have stripped him of his fake epaulets. I spent the rest of the summer explaining Mariel's absence to the customers who missed her who-gives-a-shit way of sliding their drinks onto the table, her style. Mariel's only regret: she still needed two more etched sherry glasses to finish her set.

Even before I opened the letter, I could tell by its scented beeswax seal that it was from Mariel. I was living with David, enjoying the first months of nesting, when even grocery shopping is magnetic. We would stop to buy raspberry-coconut juice or to admire the blatantly sexual squash. Once David met Mariel at a party, but all he remembered was a woman with brown hair. Mariel was plain. Above average height, dark-eyed, there was nothing to distinguish her, except an occasional accessory, like a pearl nose ring. My own dim surroundings had taken a turn for the better. I imagined her approving of our Polish circus posters, our Indian floor mats, and our Wagnerian candelabra – a full-busted, green-winged Valkyrie carved from wood.

Mariel and James, her friend Sharon, and James's friend Russ, moved to San Francisco that fall. Along the way there were failures, mechanical and human. James's jalopy, a '62 Chrysler, broke down in Salt Lake City. Sharon spoke of self-immolation at Lake Tahoe. Settling near the Presidio in an apartment too small for two, the four constantly bickered. While James half-heartedly looked for a job with a theater company, he worked for a Japanese gardener. All day he crawled in the dirt or carried burlap-swathed evergreens from truck to soil. The owner planted everything himself while James tilled the earth. It was very Biblical. Mariel was a pastry waitress in a ritzy café on Union Street that catered to young tourists. Though the pay was good, she detested the little dirndl skirts and puff-sleeved blouses. They reminded her of her D.P. photos, only now she was taller than her father was then.

Often Mariel spoke of her father, how during the war he'd hidden in the woods for six months to avoid the Russians, how at night he'd repaired trains to evacuate Lithuanian freedom fighters from the countryside, a candle his only light. He still had pitch-black hair, a droopy mustache, and fiery eyes. James was a poor imitation. Thin and frail, he could have fit inside her father like those wooden dolls

98

containing ever smaller versions. After six months of close quarters, the group split up: Sharon to be healed by a masseur schooled in herbology, Russ to a group of gay-rights street mimes. Sometimes Mariel would see him playing a flute or giving away flowers at Ghiardelli's. On Castro Street, James ran into Michael, a former lover, and decided to move in with him. Mariel showed no resentment, just spoke of cultivating a California tan, watching whales spout off the coast, and planning another trip to Germany. I didn't hear from her the rest of the year.

Men to whom I am attracted are always the physical opposite of my short, bald father. David was a towhead, a foot taller at six feet, four inches. That we were still living together after a year testified to my insight in avoiding fatherly types. By now we'd merged our checking accounts, bought a sofa with joint funds, and shared an electric typewriter. David was working in book design for a university press, and I was substituting at an alternative school for pregnant girls, when we received a postcard with the photo of a glistening herring: "Back from Germany and Scandinavia. I have my hair cut short like a boy's. I am living with a man named Roger. He's a comedian – and FUNNY!" I wrote to tell Mariel that in a few months David and I would be coming west to see my sister in Marin. Hopefully we could arrange a night on the town.

Before our trip was scheduled, I received a few more letters from Mariel, each a messy parcel of grief. Mariel had had an abortion and felt very bad. At the efficient new clinic, all aluminum and white tile, they had hurried through it. There'd been a lot of pain and blood. In the recovery room afterward, Mariel was the oldest, but despite her desire to comfort the other girls, some as young as thirteen, her screams were so loud and persistent that they had to give her a sedative. Sharon had really tried to kill herself (by Seconal rather than fire), and her mother had come all the way from Chicago to take her home. If Roger was funny, I couldn't discern his influence on Mariel's letter, except in the following detail: Sharon's mother was terrified of planes, so she'd taken Greyhound west. By the time she arrived, frantic with visions of Sharon in a locked ward or a zipped morgue bag, Sharon was feeling so much better that she refused to leave. Sharon and her mother spent the next week at Fisherman's Wharf buying all the cheap keepsakes they could load into shopping bags.

About a month later, another letter arrived, misery seeping through like a bathtub overflowing on a rug. Roger was back, working in a sporting-goods store after losing the comic lead in a play. Mariel had had a second abortion, this one a cinch compared to the first. Then Roger's adoptive mother had sent him an urgent letter. She'd received word that Roger's real father had Woody Guthrie's disease and that Roger had a fifty-percent chance of contracting it by age forty. If Mariel stayed with Roger, they could never have children. I imagined that at this rate Mariel would have twenty-four abortions before she reached menopause.

Mariel's boyish razor-cut, her new thinness, and Roger's vivacious hostility were all unanticipated. David didn't recognize Mariel at all, having remembered a different person with a nose ring from the party. Surrounded by blue-haired elders brought by sightseeing bus, stop number three, we spent the evening at Finocchio's, a slick transvestite nightclub. I kept evaluating Roger's movements for symptoms of the disease. Remembering how ravaged Woody Guthrie appeared in *Alice's Restaurant*, I gasped when Roger bumped into another table on the way to our seats. Onstage a beautiful platinum blond transvestite with real cleavage sang "Moon River" so intensely it made me nervous. The sad transvestites, those with muscles bulging under their slit gowns and fishnet hose, were saved for the chorus line. One was Chinese, petite with a waist-length fall and delicate eyelids. The face was beautiful, but the legs were wrestler's, the feet wide enough to support Rodin's statue of Balzac.

We walked around Broadway and said goodbye at the bus to the Sausalito ferry. Mariel and I had spoken little. She was wholly self-absorbed, turned inward like a clam. It might have been Mariel, rather than Roger, who was dying of something romantic and devastating. Worried for both of them, I clung to David on the ship's top deck. I felt colder than was reasonable, since the wind was still and the night air filled with warm vapor, clouding the lights on the distant hills of the bay.

David and I broke up. He accepted a book-designing job in New York and moved there on his savings, leaving me a couch and a distaste for raspberry-coconut juice. There had been no intrigue, just a gradual wearing down of the mechanism for concern. Still feeling numb and displaced, I found a job teaching English and German at a small parochial school. Grading essays on "Successful Women in Science" and eating canned gazpacho soup, I opened the first letter Mariel had sent in months. Like those colorful seed packets advertised in Sunday magazines that one never orders for fear they won't sprout, Mariel's ornate envelope was full of disappointments. Roger had gone to visit his family in Texas, where he met an old high-school girlfriend. I imagined Cybill Shepherd in *The Last Picture Show*. He had decided to stay with her. Mariel wondered whether he had made up the whole story of Woody Guthrie's disease so that she wouldn't decide to stay pregnant. Mariel was angry. She'd been tricked and didn't trust men. I sent her back a commiserating letter, telling her my own problems with David. "We're going through our petulant midtwenties. Let's seclude ourselves in the hills of Andorra and wait for wisdom." I never received an answer to the letter. Before she received it, Mariel had left for Frankfurt, where her favorite aunt was dying.

In Germany Mariel learned that her father had been an enemy of the Russians not for his freedom fighting but for his Nazi collaboration. He was still subject to extradition by the U.S. government should they uncover his activities. This secret, which Aunt Lydia had intended to take to her grave, was told to Mariel in her aunt's hospital room eleven days before she died. I imagined theatrical stage whispers, powerful organ music. Mariel promised not to tell anyone. Supposedly her mother had never known and wasn't to know. Only I knew, and the letter should be destroyed. Holding it over my Wagnerian candelabra, I turned it to ash. It seemed an appropriately dramatic gesture. At the same time I damned her for the knowledge. Kept awake by it at night, I saw her father repairing death trains by candlelight. I pictured rows of sad Jewish faces lined up at a snowy station. In my half-sleep version, Mariel's father confiscated their purses and kept the valuables, tossing the useless or sentimental onto the tracks. No wonder her mother had a boyfriend, I thought, a sad little man from church who designed surgical tools and was called Uncle by the family. No wonder her father's recent layoff from his job as a diesel mechanic was a symbol of doom, causing a two-week collapse and a nervous reunion at his bedside. Still, I assured Mariel I'd visit when I came west that summer.

The afternoon of the visit, I was in charge of my nieces, ages four and six. Lilly, the older, has black wavy hair and aquamarine eyes. Miranda is chestnut: hair, skin, eyes, warm as a sunspot on a rug. In a pink stucco apartment house we met Mariel's new boyfriend, Carlos, a wealthy Spaniard. He was working as a waiter at the St. Francis until he found the best place in the city to open a grillade. The visit came shortly after Franco's death and Prince Juan Carlos's democratization of the country. Though I knew little of Spanish politics, I had read *For Whom the Bell Tolls* and had seen *Guernica*. I expected that Carlos, whom Mariel had described as passionate and full of ideas, would be basking in his country's good fortune.

Mariel was wearing a purple silk Japanese robe. Her hair

was long again and pulled back at her temples with red combs. She had never looked more radiant. The apartment smelled of strong coffee and baking bread, the product, a braided wreath, surrounded by earthenware jars of sweet butter, jam, and honey. The other aroma was musk oil, emanating from Carlos, who, like all of Mariel's boyfriends, was short, slightly built, and handsome. His eyes were the color of Lilly's. In fact, he asked if my nieces were Spanish, for they looked like so many children in Barcelona.

"Russian and Romanian, Jewish," I answered.

In all seriousness Carlos said, "Such nice-looking people are rare here." Puzzled, I wondered if Mariel had ghoulish acquaintances.

"Carlos thinks Americans are ugly because there's so much mixing of nationalities," Mariel explained. Worse yet, I could tell she believed what she was saying. Aside from wanting to look in a mirror, I was unable to respond. I imagined dachshunds welded to Airedales, the union of a fish and a goat. My mind spun with mythological half-breeds.

The children, unaware of the tension in the dining room, munched on huge chunks of bread that Carlos tore off with his hands, tried on Mariel's straw hats, and chirped back at her canary, Liebchen. Lilly cradled a clown doll, twisting its orange straw hair. Miranda pored over the black, thickly inked wood carving in a German fairy-tale book. Afraid to probe further, I drank my coffee. When I could no longer stand my own silence, I asked Carlos how he liked the new government in Spain. "With Franco we had money. Now we have taxes, very bad for families like mine. Money is freedom." The sour feeling rose in my stomach. I wanted to take the children away. I wanted to cut myself out of the scene with the precision surgical instruments Mariel's "uncle" designed. Instead, I said a polite goodbye to Carlos when he left for work and even let him kiss my hand.

I spent a long afternoon with Mariel, listening to her reminisce about Professor Hambling, Mr. Ewell, James, Sharon,

Russ, Roger, David, Aunt Lydia, her father. I watched in-distinct shadows lengthen and consume each other. Weighed down, I couldn't have moved if the children needed me. I thought of my own father, short, bald, pale-eyed, honest, dead the same year Mariel had her abortions. For the first time in years I remembered the maple hutch where he kept his war mementos: a saucer-sized piece of shrapnel, a photo of his supply ship, before-and-after Navy-issue postcards of Nagasaki. I hoped my mother hadn't kept the grim souve-nirs after he died. I didn't want to see Mariel again. There was too much death between us. Yet as I listened to her de-scribing our times together, holding each moment up in the dim, webbed light of late afternoon, I understood. A refugee child, Mariel saved things. I was American. I wanted to throw everything away.

TWO TIMES TWO

MARIAH DAVIS WAS named after the song "They Call the Wind Mariah." Floris Davis heard it in the '42 Ford on the way to Billings Hospital to have her only daughter. Whoever called the wind such a strange and beautiful name would take notice of a baby called the same. Mariah Davis grew up uneventfully, learned to type, married at seventeen, and gave Floris Davis five grandsons: Laron, Larue, LeRoy, Lemont, and the youngest, Lebaron, named after the car his father drove for the State's Attorney.

On the day Lebaron turned eight, he couldn't wait for school to begin so it could be over. Parked at his home would be the bicycle that Floris had promised him at Christmas, if he was a good boy. And Lebaron was a good boy. His teacher, Miss Hershey (White Chocolate, some of the older boys called her), would say, "Lebaron, what is two times two?" and faithfully Lebaron answered. If Miss Hershey asked him in winter when it was snowing, the answer was four, and if she asked him before recess, the answer was the same.

That day Miss Hershey was sick with stomach flu, and a new teacher had been sent. Tall, thick, red-faced, she was the teacher voted Most Likely to Explode by every class who saw her. Her presence inspired respect. Miss Whistlestop (for that is what her name sounded like to the children) saw a flaw in the character of every student she had encountered in her twenty-four years as a substitute teacher in the public schools. At heart Miss Whistlestop was a romantic, in search of her own past, of girls in seersucker dresses with hair ribbons and boys who said, "Thank you, ma'am," even when their little arms were being twisted. Memories came back to her as light flooded into the classroom, spotlighting the chalk dust. They haunted her as she marched from the gray principal's office to Room 109. They interrupted the comment about her "white ass," spoken in the hallway. They filled her with sad longing as the little black faces of Room 109 regarded her with a painful sense of loss. So this is what happens when we're bad, they all thought, remembering their pranks and whispers. Miss Hershey's presence appeared before them like a bland angel, but she floated in another atmosphere, for when Franklin Jasper thought, "*Save us, Miss Hershey, Amen,*" nothing happened.

The morning progressed without incident, even the worst children doodling seriously in their workbooks. Miss Whistlestop spent her time far away from them, back in the fifth-grade classroom where it had been her duty and hers alone to water the sweet-potato plant. Remembering left her almost serene just before lunch time when she went to get her sandwich from the teachers' refrigerator. When her left heel followed her out the door, there was a release of air as the children sighed in unison. Lebaron whispered to Colandra Wiggens about the bicycle that awaited him. Marita Mayes took all fourteen of her doggy barrettes out of her hair and placed them in a different pattern. Others tapped with their rulers, drew on their desks, ate their paste, or picked their noses. Several of the usual troublemakers left their seats, and someone took the keys from Miss Hershey's desk drawer.

During lunch the children ate their pizza muffins and drank their free milk with the sobriety of the condemned. It was almost one o'clock, which meant a return to class. Miss Whistlestop dawdled over her turkey on rye, thinking of the American chop suey that had been her favorite in the high-school cafeteria, its gooey consistency, as if a fragrant tree had dripped sap into the simmering pot. When Miss

Whistlestop noticed it was five minutes to one and went to unlock the readers in the cabinet, Miss Hershey's keys were missing. Scenes of distress flashed before her. She would be unable to go home until the keys were found. By the time she left school, it would be dark, and she would be raped by the student who either loved or hated her white ass. Her neighborhood butcher would be closed. She'd miss her chicken breast. *Dick Van Dyke* would be over. Her cat, Gorman, named after her eighth-grade teacher, would be hungry and complaining. She would not be asked back to the Stephen Douglas School. The other teachers would comment. She was careless. She was not to be trusted.

At one o'clock when the children returned from lunch, Miss Whistlestop was outraged. Lebaron looked at her face, red as a Crayola, and thought about his bike, which would also be red, he hoped. He thought of the class party and the cookies shaped like windmills from Holland that Miss Hershey always brought on someone's birthday.

"Lebaron Wagner," Miss Whistlestop shouted as the afternoon bell rang. Lebaron raised his head hopefully, expecting to be asked the product of two times two. Four was on his tongue.

"You, to the front." He sidled up. "Who did it?" she asked, her large face so close he could feel her breath.

He had never been asked a question like that before. He remembered television shows he'd seen where women always picked men from line-ups. He thought of the time Melody Washington had been run over at recess and a black policeman, darker than anyone in his family, had asked the children on the playground for a description of the car. Lebaron had stood open-mouthed, licking his lips in excitement, as a seventh grader had created a fantastic pink Cadillac with the insignia *Ace* painted on the back window in silver letters. Lebaron had seen an unremarkable blue sedan thud against Melody, but he assumed the older children knew better the correct way to answer such a question.

Convinced that what Miss Whistlestop wanted was dramatic impact, Lebaron conjured up the meanest, ugliest man he had ever seen in a TV line-up and said, "A big dude with shades and no hair. Fatter than my daddy."

Miss Whistlestop cracked her knuckles one by one. After the last knuckle, she took Lebaron by the arm and placed him in the teacher's closet, no larger than a locker with its one hook, empty in the heat, and closed the door. One by one she called up other children, storing them in corners, on the special reading chairs, and in the adjoining cloakroom, until she found Ladora Turner, who went with the odds: "Johnny Mane done it." Right or wrong, Johnny Mane always "done it," so it was an acceptable answer. Amused in his seat at the back of the fifth row, Johnny reached into his pocket, and in a gesture of bravado that surprised even himself, sailed a set of keys past Miss Whistlestop's ear — a set of keys but not Miss Hershey's. Johnny Mane surrendered to the enraged woman who was a hundred-twenty pounds his better. Miss Whistlestop forgot the real missing keys, the imagined consequences, the banished children, and marched Johnny to the office for immediate retribution, pure and sweet.

By the time Johnny's mother had been called and the scene in the office resolved ("He could have put out my eye," Miss Whistlestop maintained), the afternoon was over. She dismissed the children and let them run down the green concrete halls when the big clock leapfrogged to three-fifteen. Locked and forgotten in the closet, Lebaron heard pounding feet and whooping and hollering that seemed so distant it might have been on another planet. He heard windows slamming shut, *thud, thud, thud,* and tried to call out, but his thin voice was lost in the bustle. Lebaron cried as Miss Whistlestop watered Miss Hershey's coleus plant and walked out the door, thinking of Miss Lyons, her second-grade teacher, who always wore nylons with seams. He banged on the varnished door, hoping Miss Whistlestop was still in the room. Then he decided that she had left him there on purpose, as punishment for giving the wrong answer. Maybe she was on her way right now to tell his grandma that he'd been bad, and the big truck that was supposed to bring his bike today would drive right past his house. Maybe it already had.

ENOUGH

LAURA LIKES TO lie down and rest in the heat of the afternoon while Matt sleeps in the next room, swathed in crochet like a large, pleasant insect. She closes the shades and turns on the old cool-jazz station and shuts her eyes. She plunges down into her bed, and even when Matt cries through the wall and she knows he is crying, she is able to stay inside, sealed off. "I'm not being a bad mother," she says, shaking her head, wiping sweat from the hairline, wondering whether Duke Ellington, who is playing now, minds that a baby is crying and that she feels serene. Once Billie Holiday sang "God Bless the Child," and Laura found herself weeping into her pillowcase. Glenn Miller strikes up "String of Pearls," and yogurt waits cold and lovely in the humming refrigerator. A kid across the street is shouting, "It's not fair!" but Laura feels light and hazy as a cloud. It's relief, like swimming underwater on a hot day. At three when the news begins, she'll comfort Matt and become a mother again, but nothing is to interrupt her hour off.

A bell rings. She thinks it is part of "Take the A Train," but no music has ever insisted so. If she doesn't answer it, if she doesn't...answer....She whirls into a sitting position, rubs her eyes, slips a terry duster over her bra and underpants, and runs down the stairs. She thinks about her unpolished toenails as they precede her into the hallway.

Through the screen door that she always locks ("Even with it locked, your life is in peril," her mother has warned. "Where do you think you live, Utopia? Consider the baby"), she sees a bald head and squinting eyes, a pale and scholarly burglar sizing up the booty. And then a voice, familiar but as hard to understand as the voice on the phone the first time she made a call in France.

"Laurie!" Harold always uses the diminutive to remind her that he is Bob's older, more brilliant brother, who was a full professor in history when Bob was still a high-school audio-visual aide with bad skin. "Anybody home?" crackles a voice behind him, invisible but unmistakably Binky's — Harold's wife, Faithful Companion, Sidekick, Comic Relief. Binky is the size of a large child, and though she is a crack archæologist, she carries on like Andy Devine, following Harold, praising his slightest effort, apologizing for his indiscretions. "Harold is sorry we didn't call first," she shouts through the screen. "We didn't have your phone number, but we remembered your address." Behind them Laura hears kids' voices, high and insistent, something about "onesies" and "backsies."

Upstairs Matt is howling. It isn't fair. It's past three, and Laura is supposed to be on duty again. She unhooks the lock and says, "Excuse me. The baby is crying."

Back in the bedroom, Laura smooths the covers, turns off the radio, and picks up Matt, raging in his crib. His skin is mottled red, and his ears smell of milk. He needs to be nursed, so Laura sits on the bed and holds him. His mouth begins sucking even before she has offered her breast, and his head bobs back and forth like a wind-up toy, blue eyes bulging, mouth furious, trying to feed on air. "Wait, wait," she consoles. "Mommy is getting ready. Here she is." And the crying turns into short tugging grunts, frantic and pitiful. She feels so sorry for Matt and for herself. The boredom of sitting still while he nurses. She wants to be reading or watching some anonymous group of ballplayers make an orderly progress around an artificially green diamond. There is something so anxious and explosive about Matt. He sucks and sucks, and Laura thinks about the yogurt and maybe a walk. "It's summer outside, Matt. We'll go to the park. You can meet other babies. Then it'll be fall, then winter. Then spring, Matt. Summer, fall, winter. Summer, fall, winter. Soon you'll be all grown, Matt, all grown, no more baby!"

"Anybody home?" Binky asks. Harold has probably sent her up to research the situation and send down a report.

"In here," Laura says and tugs Matt away from her breast. He sputters and cries and sucks at her shoulder.

"Here they are," Binky shouts to her family below. "In the bedroom, Clea. Randy, come see your new cousin." She whispers to Laura, as if whispering will help, "He's beautiful, a dream."

Laura notices that Binky has lost a canine tooth and hasn't replaced it. She thinks of Matt's pink gums, so amazingly strong. Two children built upon the same general plan shyly step into the room. Clea is ten and Randy eight, or vice versa. Binky and Harold had their children in the nick of time, Binky likes to say. Clea has a high IQ, Laura remembers from a letter. Nothing much ever gets said about Randy. She looks him up and down. He is watching himself chew gum in the mirror.

"Come up, Harold," Binky shouts. "Laura's been nursing the baby." The last detail is meant to reassure Harold that it's safe. No marauders can seize him. No one can challenge his ascendancy over the Mortons. Laura is disarmed, nursing a baby. Harold looks distracted. He eyes Matt casually and seems to reserve judgment.

"Was I that small?" Clea asks.

"Don't you remember?" Harold answers.

Laura thinks of the foolishness of his reply. Or maybe it is the beginning of their act: Dad asks Clea if she remembers being small and gifted Clea launches into the minuscule details of her infancy à la Proust. They can play literary conferences and English-department parties from coast to coast.

"No," Clea says. "How could I?"

Laura likes that. A traitor in their midst, willing to challenge Harold.

"Where's Shirlee?" Laura asks about Binky's mother, an aged ex-ballerina.

"She's too old to travel much, honey."

Randy has taken to carving his name in the velour bedspread with his index finger. "Randy Randy Randy Ran," Laura sees from vista to vista. He can spell. That much is clear.

"Her heart is enlarged," Binky adds.

Laura pictures Matt's demure heart, the size of an unfolded tulip. "Too bad," she says, for of them all Laura likes Shirlee the best, Shirlee of few words, good-natured delegate to the world at large. When Shirlee visited, she never seemed to know anyone's name or care what she was served or want for anything. Soon she'll die, Laura thinks, and assume omniscience. That's reassuring.

Too bad some of Shirlee's generous vagueness hasn't rubbed off on Harold. Laura watches him stare at her and Matt vigorously without self-consciousness. He looks like a quiz-show moderator about to ask a brilliant and difficult question. This is Harold's constant look, but the brilliant remarks are few. He saves them for his books and lectures. In fact, he's in Chicago to address yet another conference, the Society of Professors Emeritus, the theme, "Your Commitment to History." The title is elusive, another Harold strategy. Only he understands what it means. Given an hour, the audience will too, but only if they are daring enough to climb the steep sharp slopes of Harold's mind, a difficult journey for retired professors. There are no gentle hills or stairs. There is only one path, and if they don't care to follow, then they can stay in the cabin, watching the fire die. That's what Laura decided to do long ago. Laura thinks that Binky has secretly come to the same decision. She remembers asking her mother what Mrs. Santa did while Santa was delivering all the toys. "She stays at home and rests. It's her happiest night of the year."

Randy has taken to searching Laura's closet for entertainment, and Clea looks drowsy. Binky smiles blandly and pulls at Matt's little hand, which clings and tightens and flails and finally rests on Laura's shoulder. If Laura had the energy, she'd tell Binky what an infant's hand can already accomplish, what slow-motion films reveal about the apparently random movements, a strategy, an effort to grasp objects and control its world. But she is too tired.

"So where's Bob?" Harold finally asks. A trick question. As Harold knows, Bob is at the Pioneer Chemical Engineering Building, where he is every day of the year except weekends and major holidays and the three weeks he gets off for good conduct. Poor Bob, the plodding engineer, the practical one. "Whenever anything broke, Mom took it to Bob," Harold once said. "Whenever there was a *real* problem, Mom came to me." The life summed up. No way to bring back Mrs. Morton, dead twelve years now, to annotate the text. When Laura asks Bob to fix anything, no matter how simple or urgent, his reply is "Later." Then Bob secretly repairs it, but she can't see him do it or know until he is finished. It's a game they both understand. Harold only understands his own games. That's the problem with Harold.

"By the way," Harold is saying, "there's one more guest you haven't met."

Then Randy explodes out of her closet in a flurry of shoes. "Yeah, Dad. Tell her." It is a long nasal whine meant to inspire fear. Nothing they can spring on her will be worse than the sound itself. Laura feels sweat gluing her robe to her back and wipes more from her forehead. A drop falls in her eye and makes it smart.

Binky begins. "Since our last visit – when was it, a year ago Christmas – we've both added to the family. You have Matt, and we have a dog. The children really love him, but I'm afraid, as busy as we are, that he isn't well-trained."

Clea looks up at the ceiling like a guilty thug, and Randy is bouncing up and down on an invisible string. Harold has left the room to get, Laura imagines, the dog from the car, where he's already eaten the steering wheel, and bring him upstairs on cue. Before she can question, protest, or say no, in walks Harold with something yellow on a leash. It proceeds to jump up on the bed and make itself at home. Laura sees that the dog has the potential to be lovable. She sees the children still looking at her. She looks at Binky, all seersucker and good intentions, and at Harold, whose grim job it is to keep the animal at bay until Laura agrees to its presence. She imagines that at the moment when she says yes, he'll unleash the thing, and it will transform into a whirlwind of milky saliva and doggy stench.

"Okay," Laura says weakly. All she wants to do is to close her eyes, lie down in the forest of Randy's name, turn on her jazz, and sleep. She tries to summon a song, but the best she can imagine is Johnny Mathis and "Chances Are." She looks at the dog, content, panting, dozing off on the bed, and says with too much force, as if she had a position on the subject of dogs, "I don't want it on the furniture."

"Randy, honey," Binky croons, "get him off Aunt Laura's bed. Why don't you take him downstairs or go play with him in the yard? Aunt Laura has a nice yard. Clea, go with him."

Laura wishes Binky would stop calling her Aunt Laura. She doesn't want to think about that connection.

"No," Clea says and slumps back into the rattan chair, where Laura sometimes sits holding Matt. The chair has a worn area on the arm that Laura casually dissected one afternoon when every appliance in the house was broken and Bob was in a petulant mood.

"Clea," Harold says in a voice of command. Clea immediately leaves the room. The dog, leash and all, chases after her, and Randy shoots down the stairs behind. As soon as the kids are out of the room, Binky says, "Are you all right, Laura? Bob wrote that you haven't been well since the baby was born. Is it fatigue or what?"

How can she explain it? Whatever it is, it has her by the ankles and knees and thighs and stomach and chest. Sometimes her head surfaces but only to breathe in some music. Whatever it is has a firm grip and jaws. Whatever it is makes her sweat, even when it's cold, and fear Matt, even when he is peaceful and unclenched. Laura hears shouting in the back yard, Randy's voice, the dog, laughter. "It's nothing," Laura finally says. "Matt never sleeps. He has allergies."

Harold looks suspicious, like Jack Webb in *Dragnet*.

"What else did Bob say?" Laura asks. She wasn't aware that Bob had discussed her "condition" with them.

"Oh, nothing," Harold says quickly. Laura will ask Binky later, privately.

Clea and Randy are in the room. Randy is crying, and Clea is shouting, "He's gone." She shoots poison at her brother. "You shouldn't have let Randy go out with Breezer."

"What happened?" Harold booms from his throne.

"Randy disobeyed. He went in front with Breezer, and Breezer started running. I chased him for a block, but I couldn't catch up. And you know how Randy helped? He just sat there and banged his head."

"Randy is in a special school," Binky says consolingly.

Clea falls onto the bed, weeping and kicking. Randy stands like a tree rhythmically swaying. Harold leaves the room. Outside Laura hears a car door slam.

"He's going to look for Breezer," Binky reassures the children. "We're in Laura's way. Let's put our things in the guest room, and then we'll go out and look for Breezer ourselves. He can't be far."

"There is no guest room," Laura says. "Matt lives in it now. You'll have to use the basement."

"Okay," Binky says. "Come on, kids." She reminds Laura of a Girl Scout leader. They follow her out, a deflated little family leaking sweat and disappointment.

After they leave the room, she puts Matt back in his crib in the old guest room and lies down on her bed. Her eyes are heavy and sting. She closes them very gently, thinking of locking a big storage trunk, the kind her grandmother kept old hats in. She'd like to hide in one, grow small in it, and disappear. "And where is Laura?" Harold will say. "She didn't obey," Clea will answer. "She climbed into the trunk, and we can't get her out."

The next voice Laura hears is Bob's. She opens her eyes to see him frowning down on her. He looks tired and wet and has a leaf caught in his hair. He looks so disheveled that Laura wonders if he has swung home from work through the dark shiny cottonwoods that snow on their yard whenever a strong wind blows.

"Why are you asleep?"

"Because I'm tired."

"We have guests," Bob is saying through his teeth. "Can't you be right?"

"Did they find the dog?" Laura asks.

"What dog?"

"The one that ran away."

Bob is irritated that he doesn't understand. "Do you think you can get up?"

Laura closes her eyes. No, there isn't a chance that she can get up. She will stay in bed forever. "I'm very tired," Laura says and closes her eyes. Laura sings to herself "In My Solitude."

When she is finished singing, she counts silently to fifty backward and forward. When she opens her eyes, Bob will be gone.

"What are you doing?" he asks. "Do I have to call your mother?"

"Why would you?" Laura asks feebly.

Each word feels as if it can't escape whole, as if it might

break, so she whispers, but now she can't stop whispering. Binky is stroking her brow and saying, "Okay, honey, you rest, you rest," but Laura isn't listening.

She is falling deeper and deeper into her bed. She is smaller and smaller. She is floating under turquoise water, a shimmering tan shape contracting and relaxing, contracting and relaxing, to the sound of a straining clarinet.

RESPECT
FOR THE DEAD

SUSAN FOLLOWED THE smell of incense down the dark hall to apartment F. She knocked softly, holding her breath between knocks. Rodney couldn't be expected to look or act like anyone else she knew, not even Rodney. She remembered them sitting in his bedroom on a hot day in August twenty years ago. She was twelve and Rodney ten. The room was sweltering, but Rodney appeared unaware of discomfort. Besides, they were playing "Underwater," and the heat provided the scenario. Hal couldn't understand her curiosity about her utterly lost cousin, hospitalized in a home for years. Ever since she heard he was in the city, Susan breathed Rodney.

"He's crazy, Susan, certified," Hal said, pulling up his socks.

"He was crazy when we were kids. That's why we had so much fun."

"Why do you want to see him now? To feel depressed?"

"On the contrary," Susan said, sounding defensive. "Rodney is my flesh and blood, my closest cousin. We looked alike when we were children." Convenient sentiments. "Besides, he's right in the neighborhood."

Hal pursued, his eyes fixing hers, a tactic he employed when he thought he was winning. "There are plenty of weirdos in the neighborhood, but you don't pass your time visiting halfway houses."

Susan knocked again. No answer. "Rodney?" She heard a stirring behind the door, like a mouse burrowing under newspaper. "Rodney, it's your cousin Susan. Are you in there?"

"Rather."

"Rather?" Susan shouted at the door. The man in E, wearing a ski cap pulled over his ears, cracked open his door and peered out. "He's my cous — " she began explaining but was interrupted by a slamming and the clasping of three chains.

"Rodney, should I come back another time? Or would you like to visit me instead? I have a daughter. Her name is Elizabeth. She looks like you."

"Are you vegetarians?" the voice asked.

"Not really, Rodney, but I could make a spinach salad." Immediately she felt foolish.

"Is Beatrice out there?"

"Your mother? No, she's not even alive. I just saw your neighbor in E, though."

"Do you vote?"

"Usually, but Hal never does. He says it's boring. Did you know I married Hal?" Susan heard a stirring.

"Care for some water?"

"No thank you, Rodney."

"Mind if I do?"

"Please go ahead."

Susan looked in her purse, took out a yellow-rimmed mirror, and tried to see Rodney in her face. When she was in college, Rodney — already "not right," as her mother euphemized — came to visit her. During gym class, he approached her on the badminton court, shuttlecocks whizzing past his ears. They'd had a long conversation, Rodney confessing he'd been ill, but now he was considering flying school.

"Rodney, can I come in?"

No answer. "Remember when we stole sunglasses from all those parked cars and had to put them back and couldn't find the right cars, so we just put them anywhere?" No answer. "And remember when Bubi would talk to you in

Yiddish and you'd answer in pig Latin? And remember....
And remember...." Susan couldn't stop. "Rodney, will you
let me see you?" Her mother had said that in the hospital
he kept by his bed a dime-store picture of a woman he didn't
know. "Rodney? I'll slip my phone number under the door.
Call me."

That night Elizabeth was coloring in her bedroom, and Hal
and Susan were sitting in front of their finished meals,
drinking wine. Susan chewed on a chicken bone, thinking
of Rodney's door.
    "So how did it go?"
    "What?"
    "Your visit with Rodney, the one who's afraid to eat be-
cause he feels guilty about tomatoes."
    "He asked me if we're vegetarians."
    "A holier-than-thou nut."
    "He also asked me if we voted. I told him you didn't."
    "Why did you tell him *that*?"
    "Because you don't."
    "How does he look? Just like you?"
    "Oh, he seemed well. He asked me if Beatrice was with
me. Hal, we used to talk pig Latin together."
    "Mommy, the phone is for you. It's a man. He won't talk
to me." Elizabeth, carrying one brown crayon, looked de-
feated.
    "Hello?"
    "Is this Susan?"
    "Rodney?"
    "Can you do me a favor?"
    "Sure, what is it?"
    "Can you drive me to the cemetery?"
    "Why do you want to go there?"
    "To see my mother. I was away when she died."
    "Okay. How about tomorrow at noon? Maybe we can
go out to lunch too."

"Just the cemetery."

"Okay, I'll pick you up at your place."

"Goodbye."

Before Susan could say goodbye, Rodney had hung up. She went back in the dining room and started clearing away dishes. Susan remembered Rodney's bedroom, where he invented space machines made of rubber bands, paper clips, Popsicle sticks. His bare walls. The science-fiction books he hid under his bed as though they were contraband. Hal wouldn't know her plans this time.

"Who was it?"

"Elizabeth's school, a board meeting."

The next day at twelve, Susan pulled up in front of Rodney's building. An elderly man with sunglasses stood in front, trying to pelt a dog too far away to hit with the stones. The dog was mangy and walked sideways. Susan was sure it lived there too. The door opened, and a slumped, slim figure approached. He wore a white dress shirt, no tie, and jeans. Susan looked at his face and saw Rodney as she'd remembered.

Without acknowledging her, he got in the car. He smelled of incense. His job in the halfway house was packaging incense, the product of their cottage industry. A blend of sandalwood, patchouli, and evergreen consumed the air in the car. Susan opened the window.

"Close it," Rodney said.

"But it's hot in here."

"It's dangerous."

"You look well, Rodney. I'm happy to see you." Susan reached for his hand. He pulled it away without looking at her.

"Look," he said, holding out a wooden ladle.

Susan nodded at him, thinking of what to say.

"It was my mother's."

"My mother has one too." Rodney looked in the back seat, as if Susan were addressing someone who was hidden.

"Sure you don't want lunch?"

"I don't eat food."

"How about some coffee or tea?" Susan imagined Rodney sitting in the dark, munching on a hidden salami.

"They're dangerous."

"Well then, it's a long ride to the cemetery. Should I turn on the radio?" She knew by now she'd better ask.

"Respect for the dead," Rodney said, pointing out the window. Susan saw a sign for fresh fish.

"I remember going out here a lot as a child," she said. "My parents would place plants that looked like cabbages on graves of people I never knew. It always made me sleepy. I haven't been out here since my father died. Did you know my father died?"

"Your father?"

"Yes."

"No," Rodney nodded his head again and again in the affirmative.

Susan handed him her wallet. "Open it up. I have pictures of Hal and Elizabeth."

Rodney held it at a distance from his body, inspecting it for hazards. He opened the wallet and looked in her change purse. "Here. Money's dirty."

"I guess it is," Susan agreed. "Would you like to meet Hal and Elizabeth some time?"

Rodney sighed. It was the beginning of a silence, heavy as incense, that lasted until they arrived at the cemetery.

Westlake was one of the Jewish cemeteries on the outskirts of the city. Built at a time when farms bordered its edges, it now intruded on an Italian neighborhood on one side and a forest preserve on the other. It was divided into sections with picturesque names that seemed descriptive of nothing:

Pine Ridge, Weeping Willow, Blue Jay. You needed a map to get around. Susan took the official map from the guard. Rodney stared at the dashboard.

"Your mother's over here, I think. In Green Knoll. She's buried with her parents."

No answer.

Susan drove slowly over the winding streets arranged in a cloverleaf. There were several other cars and in one section a funeral in progress. A green canopy had been erected over the burial site, and from their distance the mourners looked like waiting commuters.

"We're almost there." Susan parked the car at the curb. "Would you like to go alone, or should I come along?"

No reply.

"Rodney, this is where your mother's buried. Do you want to see her grave?"

"You go," he said.

Susan looked worried. "Okay, I'll be right back. You'll wait here?"

No answer. Susan looked at Rodney, trying to meet his eyes, remembering a pact they'd sworn not to show her mother the stolen decoder he had given her. Rodney stared at the instrument panel as if it were giving him secret instructions.

Susan walked through the grass to Beatrice Groman, 1916–1972. She didn't know how long Rodney wanted her to stand there, how long would be sufficient to prove she was at rest despite her youngest son. Susan looked up at the sky. She thought she saw a jet overhead, but at this distance it looked like a single red dot sliding through blue. She thought of the painting she had finished, of Elizabeth asking her why she never painted farms. "Because I can't draw animals." She heard a noise like a car starting. It *was* a car starting. Susan looked over to the curb and saw Rodney in the driver's seat, hands intent on the wheel. She ran through the grass, trying to step over the gravestones and still get there in time. Rodney accelerated and drove off when Susan was even with the Geller family plot. She stood there, heart pounding, next to an unmarked grave.

Slowly she walked down the road to the cemetery office. She thought of alerting the people attending the funeral, but it was too ridiculous. "Damn him, damn Beatrice." The guard would call a cab for her, she thought, checking her purse to see if she had the fare. "Damn him." She'd have to tell Hal.

The cab ride home was a blank. The driver, an elderly black man, didn't try to make conversation. A woman who took a seventeen-dollar cab ride home from a cemetery deserved her privacy. When they pulled up in front of Susan's apartment, a police car was waiting.

A young blond policeman with mustard around one side of his mouth said, "Your husband's at the station. I'll take you there. He wants to know if you want to press charges."

"Press charges?"

"Yes, auto theft. We already have him on reckless driving and driving without a license."

"Rodney?"

"A Mr. Groman, ma'am."

"Was he injured? How's the car?"

"No injuries. The car sustained minor damage. You shouldn't leave your keys in the car like that, ma'am. You don't realize the dangerous element out loose. The other week a woman on Pine Grove left her keys in the door to her apartment while she brought in the groceries. When she closed the door, some maniac was waiting for her with a hammer."

"Did she get away?"

"I can't discuss the case further, ma'am."

Susan's head hurt. She didn't want to see Rodney *or* Hal. "Is he at the station?"

"The accused is in lock-up. He had no identification, but he says he's a Mr. Groman."

The policeman was already out of the car, unlocking Susan's door. Hal stood on the station steps, an unofficial sentry.

"Well, Miss Bleeding Heart?"

"Did you see him, Hal? Is he okay?"

"He won't see anybody. The story he tells is that he stole a stranger's car at the cemetery. A *stranger*, Susan. He said he walked there."

Susan looked down at the gray monumental stairs. She had never been at a police station before. She remembered that Rodney had once asked her if she'd be his friend, even when they were old. "I'll always be your cousin," she had said.

VINTAGE
CONTEMPORARIES

___ **Love Always** by Ann Beattie	$5.95	74418-7
___ **First Love and Other Sorrows** by Harold Brodkey	$5.95	72970-6
___ **The Debut** by Anita Brookner	$5.95	72856-4
___ **Cathedral** by Raymond Carver	$4.95	71281-1
___ **Bop** by Maxine Chernoff	$5.95	75522-7
___ **Dancing Bear** by James Crumley	$5.95	72576-X
___ **One to Count Cadence** by James Crumley	$5.95	73559-5
___ **The Wrong Case** by James Crumley	$5.95	73558-7
___ **The Last Election** by Pete Davies	$6.95	74702-X
___ **A Narrow Time** by Michael Downing	$6.95	75568-5
___ **Days Between Stations** by Steve Erickson	$6.95	74685-6
___ **Rubicon Beach** by Steve Erickson	$6.95	75513-8
___ **A Fan's Notes** by Frederick Exley	$7.95	72915-3
___ **A Piece of My Heart** by Richard Ford	$5.95	72914-5
___ **The Sportswriter** by Richard Ford	$6.95	74325-3
___ **The Ultimate Good Luck** by Richard Ford	$5.95	75089-6
___ **Fat City** by Leonard Gardner	$5.95	74316-4
___ **Within Normal Limits** by Todd Grimson	$5.95	74617-1
___ **Airships** by Barry Hannah	$5.95	72913-7
___ **Dancing in the Dark** by Janet Hobhouse	$5.95	72588-3
___ **November** by Janet Hobhouse	$6.95	74665-1
___ **Fiskadoro** by Denis Johnson	$5.95	74367-9
___ **The Stars at Noon** by Denis Johnson	$5.95	75427-1
___ **Asa, as I Knew Him** by Susanna Kaysen	$4.95	74985-5
___ **A Handbook for Visitors From Outer Space** by Kathryn Kramer	$5.95	72989-7
___ **The Chosen Place, the Timeless People** by Paule Marshall	$6.95	72633-2
___ **Suttree** by Cormac McCarthy	$6.95	74145-5
___ **The Bushwhacked Piano** by Thomas McGuane	$5.95	72642-1
___ **Nobody's Angel** by Thomas McGuane	$6.95	74738-0
___ **Something to Be Desired** by Thomas McGuane	$4.95	73156-5
___ **To Skin a Cat** by Thomas McGuane	$5.95	75521-9
___ **Bright Lights, Big City** by Jay McInerney	$5.95	72641-3
___ **Ransom** by Jay McInerney	$5.95	74118-8
___ **River Dogs** by Robert Olmstead	$6.95	74684-8
___ **Norwood** by Charles Portis	$5.95	72931-5
___ **Clea & Zeus Divorce** by Emily Prager	$6.95	75591-X
___ **A Visit From the Footbinder** by Emily Prager	$6.95	75592-8
___ **Mohawk** by Richard Russo	$6.95	74409-8
___ **Anywhere But Here** by Mona Simpson	$6.95	75559-6
___ **Carnival for the Gods** by Gladys Swan	$6.95	74330-X
___ **Myra Breckinridge and Myron** by Gore Vidal	$8.95	75444-1
___ **The Car Thief** by Theodore Weesner	$6.95	74097-1
___ **Taking Care** by Joy Williams	$5.95	72912-9

V I N T A G E
C O N T E M P O R A R I E S

"Today's novels for the readers of today." — VANITY FAIR

"Real literature—originals and important reprints—in attractive, inexpensive paperbacks." — THE LOS ANGELES TIMES

"Prestigious." — THE CHICAGO TRIBUNE

"A very fine collection." — THE CHRISTIAN SCIENCE MONITOR

"Adventurous and worthy." — SATURDAY REVIEW

"If you want to know what's on the cutting edge of American fiction, then these are the books you should be reading."
— UNITED PRESS INTERNATIONAL

On sale at bookstores everywhere, but if otherwise unavailable, may be ordered from us. You can use this coupon, or phone (800) 638-6460.

Please send me the Vintage Contemporaries books I have checked on the reverse. I am enclosing $ _____ (add $1.00 per copy to cover postage and handling). Send check or money order—no cash or CODs, please. Prices are subject to change without notice.

NAME _____

ADDRESS _____

CITY _____ STATE _____ ZIP _____

Send coupons to:
RANDOM HOUSE, INC., 400 Hahn Road, Westminster, MD 21157
ATTN: ORDER ENTRY DEPARTMENT
Allow at least 4 weeks for delivery.

005   38

ABOUT THE AUTHOR

Maxine Chernoff's poems and stories have appeared in many magazines, including the *Paris Review, TriQuarterly, North American Review,* and *Partisan Review.* She is the recipient of a Carl Sandburg Award for Poetry and a P.E.N. Syndicated Fiction Award, among other prizes. Ms. Chernoff lives in Chicago with her husband and three children, and is at work on a novel.